THE LURE
OF SWEET DEATH

By Sarah Kemp

THE LURE OF SWEET DEATH
NO ESCAPE
OVER THE EDGE

THE LURE
OF SWEET
DEATH

SARAH KEMP

PUBLISHED FOR THE CRIME CLUB BY
DOUBLEDAY & COMPANY, INC.
GARDEN CITY, NEW YORK
1986

All of the characters in this book
are fictitious, and any resemblance
to actual persons, living or dead,
is purely coincidental.

Library of Congress Cataloging-in-Publication Data

Butterworth, Michael, 1924–
The lure of sweet death.

I. Title.
PR6052.U9L87   1986   823′.914   85–27452
ISBN 0-385-19999-6

THE LURE
OF SWEET DEATH

The killer walked briskly down Laburnum Drive in the crisp March afternoon.

He had the build of an athlete gone slightly to fat, but his movements were still precise, well-coordinated, decisive. When he came to The Hollies, he took a quick look to left and right, watchful for twitching curtains, kids playing in front gardens, that kind of thing. Satisfied, he opened the gate and went up to the front door. The bell-push produced a ring of chimes; presently a woman opened up.

"Oh—hello, Norman. You're right on time. Come on in. I've got the kettle on the boil." She was in her late fifties and still handsome.

"How are you feeling, Alice?" he asked, following her down the narrow passageway that led to the kitchen. A widow living alone, she had made the kitchen the centre of her life, and apart from her bedroom, the rest of the two-storey detached villa was unused, swept clean, dusted and polished: like a folk museum.

"No worse," she responded. She used it as a sort of joke: a catch-phrase.

"I thought how well you looked when you opened the door."

She did not reply, but went on in and crossed to the sink, where a large teapot, cups and saucers, and the rest were laid out.

"Sit you down, Norman dear. I'll just heat up the kettle again."

She had her back to him and was putting tea into the pot. He looked about the small kitchen, neat as ever. On the mantelpiece was a snapshot of her and her late husband taken on a cruise to the Balearic Islands—so she had told him—the year before Ernest started his fatal illness. Next to it was a coloured postcard depicting the Sacred Heart. An

American clock ticked stridently on the wall above. Ten minutes past three, and it was already beginning to get dark.

"Did you go to the bank, Alice?" he asked.

Her hand paused in the act of reaching out to pick up the kettle, and she did not look round when she replied. "Well, I was going to talk to you about that, Norman. I drew out the money, but I've decided not to go along with you."

"Oh, Alice. After all your promises . . ."

She turned to face him, and saw the disappointment in his eyes, which were of a baby blue, and guileless.

"I told you about the offer from my sister and her hubby, didn't I, Norman? Well, I've decided it would be more proper—you know what I mean?—to go and live with them." She turned and, having poured the hot water into the pot, gave a good stir to the awakening brew within. "I like you very much, Norman, and I know you like me too. Since we first met, I think there's a real love grown up between us. Only, like I said, I've changed my mind about going along with . . ."

He was no longer listening to her. Silently rising, he tiptoed the three paces that separated them, his stubby, muscular hands outstretched.

"It *is* two sugars for you, isn't it, Norman?"

She had no time to cry out. One hand to the base of her skull, the other enclosing the chin. He gave one swift jerk to the right, so that her suddenly shocked eyes were staring at him. The neck snapped with a sharp crack like a breaking stick.

He held the body upright till the brief twitching stopped, and then lowered it to the floor. He did not look back as he went out of the kitchen and closed the door behind him.

Upstairs, in her neat bedroom, with its faded femininity—pink-striped wallpaper, the crinolined lady doll on the dressing table, a framed popular print hung above the bedhead, and the cloying scent of talcum powder—he went straight over to the suitcase that lay on the candlewick coverlet of the bed.

It was still unlocked. Opening the lid, he threw aside the neatly folded clothes and came upon a thick envelope bearing the logo of a High Street bank.

It was stuffed with twenty-pound notes. He counted a hundred.

Two thousand quid—not bad for an afternoon's work, plus a few hours' ground bait. More than he had ever made at the old game.

ONE

"Murder!"

"I'm not going to admit to that." The answer was defiant but cool.

The interrogator persisted, leaning forward and pointing. "You said—a few moments ago, you admitted . . ."

"You're twisting my words—what I said was . . ."

"It's all on record, Doctor." Jakeman allowed a note of gloating triumph to enter his voice, which, along with his sneering expression was his strongest card and he knew it: the man whom everyone loved to hate. "If you like, I'll have it played back to you."

"There's no need," came the reply. "I'll repeat it. The bite marks to the neck, the semi-strangulation—these pointed only to a passionate encounter. And the absence of blood or skin under the fingernails indicated that she had made no attempt to defend herself against this unknown man. But I was going to add—*if you hadn't interrupted me*—that I found enough barbiturate in the stomach to indicate that she'd taken an overdose of sleeping capsules three hours after the encounter, when no doubt her unknown lover had left her for good, and she decided to take her life."

First a shot of Jakeman's look of dismay—then they zoomed in on the strikingly attractive young woman in the big leather armchair, ash blond, cool, and with an assured elegance. A ghost of a smile played at the corners of her lips.

"Cut! Thank you, Tina. Thank you, Toby."

Fifteen million viewers would sigh gladly to see the triumph of Beauty over Beast as the credits began to roll up over a long close shot of the star of the show.

THE PATHOLOGIST

. . .

Cases based on the
files of Dr. Tina May,
pathologist and sleuth.

. . .

DR. TINA
was interrogated by
TOBY JAKEMAN

While all the cases are purely fictional and the persons described bear no resemblance to persons living or dead, the forensic details are strictly accurate and are of the kind that Dr. Tina meets with daily in her astonishing career . . .

"Well done, Tina. Come and have a drink."

Producer Simon Elles slipped his arm round her waist and led her in the direction of the Hospitality Room. She allowed Elles the implied intimacy—just as she owed him so much else.

"Dr. Tina, may I have your autograph, please?" This was the secretary to one of the production assistants. "It's for my little niece."

Tina scribbled her signature. They—the P.R. people—had told her to abandon her crisp, legible italic hand for a fuzzy squiggle. ("More in the image of the friendly neighbourhood G.P. who fills out your viewers' forms for pink medicine and hearing aids, darling.")

"How are you enjoying fame, Tina?" asked Elles, who, observing her slight smile of private amusement, totally misconstrued it.

"My bank manager took me out to lunch the other day," she replied.

"I like it—I *like* it!" guffawed Elles.

The Hospitality Room was quite crowded. They were drifting away from the monitor, where the last of the "Pathologist" credits were fading out, and were going to-

wards a tall figure in tweeds who was holding on his gauntleted wrist what Tina May perceived to be some kind of
hawk. As she and Ellis went across the unoccupied centre of
the room, the creature, discerning movement in a formerly
empty space, flicked round its beaked profile and regarded
them piercingly with wide, yellow-irised eyes. So did everyone else's eyes:

"Tina, that was great—marvellous!"

"It gets better—really riveting, darling!"

"You and Toby are a—sort of—um—sexual bouilla-
baisse . . ."

"Toby's image has *so* deteriorated. Gets proposals by the
sackful . . ."

Hand on her elbow, Elles guided her through the syco-
phants.

"Tina, this is Jamie Farrell, who runs some kind of falconry
farm. Farrell, I scarcely need to introduce the famous Dr.
Tina."

"How do you do, Mr. Farrell."

"Pleased to meet you." His manner was stiff and defensive, yet he was good-looking in a rugged, Viking sort of way.
The bird on his fist raised its wings and beat the air alarm-
ingly—but was calmly stilled by a gentle touch of his other
hand upon its speckled breast feathers.

"I'll get you the usual, Tina," said Elles. "Can I bring you
another of the same, Farrell? Half of bitter, was it?"

"Not for me," was the brusque response. "Can't play
around with a hawk when you've been boozing. They know
as soon as they look at you."

"Really? How jolly interesting." Unobserved by Farrell,
Elles hunched his shoulders and pulled a long lip at Tina as
he left them alone together; put off by the bird's apparent
savagery, the others had already moved away.

"He's very beautiful," said Tina, advancing a tentative
hand towards the bird's breast; immediately withdrawing it
as, beak slightly open, it shrank away and gathered up its
wings as if about to beat the air again.

"It's a she," said Farrell. "They're bigger than the tiercel —that's the male bird. And keener hunters." He soothed the hawk, as before.

"Is she quite young?"

"She's fresh-taken from the nest this year. What we call an eyas, and untrained. But she eats from the fist and's settling down nicely."

"And what do you call her?"

"Baby."

"Baby, that's nice. And now she's going to appear on TV with you?"

He grunted. "What they call a 'spot' on tomorrow's one o'clock magazine programme. It's not much, but it's well paid. There's no money in falconry."

"I'm sure you'll both be a hit," said Tina, and wished she hadn't sounded so patronising. But compounded it by adding: "Then everyone will point to you in the street, and you'll never know any privacy again—till they go off you, and you become an ordinary person once more."

He looked at her for the first time with something like interest.

"Do you enjoy being famous?" he asked.

The second time that question had been put to her in almost as many minutes—and about the fiftieth time that week!

"Oh yes," she replied. "Mind you, I'm going through what they call 'the honeymoon period,' when it's nice to be able to pay off all one's bills and still have some left over. And one quite likes being asked for one's autograph." She smiled. "It's an odd fact that so many of them think they're rather demeaning themselves by asking, so they say it's for their little daughter, their niece, or the like."

He didn't approve of her deliberate flippancy, for he looked at her seriously.

"You're a woman in a dedicated profession," he said. "Doesn't it ever strike you that you're cheapening yourself and your calling by reducing it to a catchpenny show on the goggle-box?"

Tina deliberately counted up to three before responding: "As to my profession," she said, "I practise it full time—as I always have and always shall. Regarding the 'catchpenny show,' as you call it: that, or something like it, was devised by Dr. John Kettle, who was my teacher, mentor, and the dearest friend of my life. Johnny's dead now, as you may or may not know—but nothing he ever engaged himself upon in all his long and notable career was ever cheap. And what was good enough for him's good enough for me."

"Quite a speech, Dr. May," responded Farrell. "I imagine you make a formidable adversary when roused. And a very loyal friend. I'd sooner have you on my side than against me."

She managed a smile. "Thank you," she said. "And I hope you and Baby enjoy your spot on the magazine programme, Mr. Farrell. She really is very beautiful. Good day to you."

She turned—and nearly bumped into Simon Elles, who was coming up with her drink.

"Leaving already, Tina?" he asked, dismayed.

"I must, Simon," she said. "Sorry—but I have to go and cheapen my dedicated profession by cutting up a dead body." This with a swift, cool glance at the man with the hawk.

Outwardly cool she might be, but the inner heat had not subsided till the taxi had borne her half-way to Lochiel Street—and that was ridiculous, for she hated losing her temper even slightly; and the man Farrell, in spite of his uncompromising attitudes, was obviously deeper water than he appeared and, away from a milieu he plainly despised, probably more agreeable, too. She would look in at the one o'clock show tomorrow.

In this calmer frame of mind, she paid off the cabbie outside the small terraced house in Chelsea that held so many memories for her. The bit about the post-mortem was a slight exaggeration: she wasn't due at the mortuary till four o'clock.

She let herself in. "Yoo-hoo, Maggie!" she called. "I'm back."

That was another plus about being a celebrity and augmenting one's income in an astonishing leap and bound: it would have taken her years of struggle to have been able to afford a full-time, living-in secretary, not to mention a word-processor and other administrative hardwear, plus a lavish conversion of the second floor back, to accommodate a new study and an office. This she had managed to accomplish from the proceeds of the first cheque upon signing the "Pathologist" contract.

"You're early, Tina. What happened to the three-hour lunch at the Café Royal?"

"Oh, I left before anyone made the offer. What's new, Maggie?"

Maggie Wainwright—petite, bespectacled, what the French call *une jolie laide,* and with a stunning figure—had no need of a clipboard; her mind was her clipboard. She rattled off the items:

"The P.M.'s been put forward to three, so it's a good thing you didn't get caught up in a protracted lunch. Jeremy Cook rang, also someone from the *Daily Journal* who wants a quote from you about AIDS—he'll ring back later. French TV want you to appear on a panel next Thursday, but I said you were booked up that day—and anyhow, your French isn't up to it. I'm having a low-calorie prawn salad for lunch—care to join me?"

"That would be nice. What did Jeremy want?" Tina kicked off her shoes and slumped down in the kitchen's best easy chair. Simultaneously, a large ginger tabby cat of villainous appearance leapt nimbly out of its basket by the radiator and in three swift bounds that belied his age and gross embon-point reaccommodated himself on her lap.

"Oh, hello, You," she said, ruffling the fur under his chin.

"He wants you to meet him for lunch tomorrow, 'cos he's got something important to tell you. You're free, so I accepted with many thanks on your behalf. By the way, I fancy that the cat over the garden wall's in season. You has been making his presence known by other than sight and sound all morning. Why did you take him on, Tina?"

"I didn't. He took me on. Simply marched in and staked out his territory—which included me."

"He's a monster."

"Yes, he is. My nightmare's to be married to a man like him. Come to think of it," she added reflectively, "I once was. Do you suppose, Maggie, that You, here, could be some kind of metamorphosis of Jock, my ex? I'm kidding, of course."

Maggie did not answer, but addressed herself to peeling the fresh prawns and casting an eye to make sure that the newly made mayonnaise had not curdled. She had heard all about the legendary Jock, who had inhabited the top floor of the house long after Tina and he had divorced; how even after that, Tina had borne with his drunkenness, his financial importunities, his crazy money-making schemes that never got off the ground—and all because of a marriage vow gone sour, and on account of a half-digested belief that, but for her, Jock's undoubted talent as a writer might have come to full promise.

"Personally, I think you should marry Jeremy Cook," said Maggie. "He dotes on you, you know he does. And Claud says he's got a great future ahead of him if ever he got married and stopped chasing a fortune at chemmy and roulette, not to mention the sort of women who'd never be of use to him in a million years." Claud was Maggie's older brother, who was also at the Bar: a prematurely old thirty-five with his eye firmly fixed on an early seat on the bench.

Tina let the issue pass without comment. They ate their prawn salad, which was superb. Afterwards Tina had a lie-down with a book, after setting her beeper for two-fifteen, at which time she got up, fixed her face and hair, grabbed her bag and brief case, and went out, calling goodbye to Maggie.

The latter shouted down the stairwell after her: "What'll I say to the *Courier* when they ring about the quote on AIDS?"

"Give them a precis of the new government handout, Maggie, and tell them that I endorse it. 'Bye."

She shut the front door behind her and went to find a taxi in the King's Road.

The Borough District Mortuary had been the last word when it was built in the 1930s, but had not caught up with the progress of pathology since. Tina changed in a cubicle the size of a shower cabinet. A plainclothes police officer was waiting for her in the lobby when she came out in a white gown, her ash-blond curls crisply tucked into a theatre cap. She recognised him as one Detective Sergeant Turner whom she had met briefly once before.

"Afternoon, Doctor," he greeted her.

"Hello, Sergeant. What's the score?"

"Well, ma'am, you might think we're romancing a little bit, but I was there when my chief made the on-the-spot investigation, and I go along with his—well—very tentative speculation."

"Which is? . . ."

They were walking together slowly down the long tiled corridor that led to the post-mortem room.

"The subject, Miss Clarice Waterhouse, aged forty-five, resided in a nice terrace house in the better part of Tooting. Her father, a wholesale fruiterer, left her a tidy sum of money. We've established that she drew out what was for her an unusually large sum from her current account—two hundred and fifty pounds—three days before her death." He gave what was obviously intended to be a significant pause.

"Go on, Sergeant," said Tina.

"When I say three days before her death, ma'am, I mean three days before her body was discovered, which was yesterday. Lying in the bath at her home. Drowned." Turner had sharp features, quizzical eyes, and a way of looking at his addressee for confirmation of his line of argument. "Does that suggest anything to you, ma'am?"

Tina returned his gaze and raised an eyebrow. "Do you have a brides-in-the-bath scenario in mind, Sergeant?" she asked. "What was the name of that famous mass-murderer?"

Turner gave a sketchy approximation to a grin. "George Smith, ma'am. Bit before your time—and mine, too. Killed three women after taking their savings by promise of marriage or bigamous marriage. I tell you, ma'am," he added, as they paused by the P.M. room door, "if this was 1915, with the evidence we already have, that woman in there"—he jerked his thumb at the door—"would be categorised as a victim of the said Smith. Motive, opportunity, *modus operandi* —identical."

"Well—we'll see what the P.M. turns up," said Tina. "Are you coming to watch?"

"Of course, ma'am," said Turner. "I can give you a lead on a few points." He looked rather uneasy. "The way things have turned out for me in my job, I've never attended a post-mortem. Got to start sometime."

The body was laid out on the drainage slab, uncovered and nude. The duty attendant was an old fellow named Thursby, whom Tina had worked with before. They exchanged the time of day, and then she regarded the corpse and made mental notes:

Mid forties . . . well nourished . . . appendectomy scar . . . clear signs of drowning and asphyxia . . . no bruises so far as I can see . . .

"Let's turn her over, Mr. Thursby," she murmured.

No bruises to the back . . . still, one wouldn't suffer bruising on a suave surface like the inside of a bath, even if one struggled . . .

She picked up the decedent's right leg by the foot and examined the ankle and lower calf.

"You won't find any bruises there, either, Doctor," said Turner, with the air of someone who has things figured out. "But there needn't be, you see. When I tell you that me and the Chief Inspector, we staged a drowning like the brides-in-the-bath case right in the shower room at the Police Sports Centre, with me stripped off in the bath and him acting out George Smith, and he took my ankles and lifted up my legs so's my head went under—you wouldn't believe! I felt nothing at all—no violence. He could have taken my ankles between finger and thumb and had me under water. No effort needed. I was helpless—*helpless!* And bloody glad when they lifted me out again—begging your pardon, ma'am."

Tina nodded. "Mmmm. By the way, did she have a regular doctor—and was he summoned?"

"No, ma'am." Turner was quite firm about that. "Miss Waterhouse had no relations, but the neighbours were very clear about her habits and character. Kept herself to herself. Took no part in the community life. And no regular doctor. No doctor at all, so far as we've been able to establish to date."

"Well," said Tina. "There's nothing left but to go in and see what we can find—if anything."

Turner sat in the waiting room of the mortuary, smoking hard and inhaling deeply. An hour had passed since he had excused himself from the sight of that beautiful woman going about her work—indeed, he had nearly fainted when, with one clean slice from throat to groin she had eviscerated the corpse. An ashtray full of cigarette butts bore mute witness to the state of mind—and memory—he had passed through since then.

He'd made a right fool of himself in there. She must be laughing at him. But how could anybody get around to being casual and workaday about a job like that? Being a copper was bad enough, particularly in the Traffic Section, having to be first on the scene in motorway pile-ups and suchlike. Not that he'd had any experience, even, of that—having spent most of his time in Criminal Records before his recent transfer to the C.I.D. Turner lit another cigarette and was pleased to see that his hands were quite steady. Still, it had certainly given him a turn . . .

He heard the tap-tap of her heels in the corridor outside. She came in, fresh as a daisy in her smart tweed two-piece, as if she'd been out for a brisk walk across the park with the dog.

He got to his feet and eyed her questioningly.

"It was suicide," she said.

He looked disappointed; she could scarcely forbear to smile.

"Are you sure, ma'am?" he asked. "Pardon me for asking."

"The stomach contained Seconal in a fatal dosage, together with shards of the capsules that led me to it. The woman took a fair handful of the things in a hot bath and slipped under the water when she became unconscious. The actual cause of death was asphyxia, which was apparent at first sight.

"And one can make a fair guess as to why she did it."

"Yes, ma'am?"

"She was suffering from fairly advanced carcinoma of the oesophagus. Cancer of the throat."

"Oh!" Turner thought for a while, then he added: "But that doesn't account for the two hundred and fifty pounds she drew out before she died. It's not been found yet, nor explained away."

Tina nodded sympathetically. "Well, that's your province, not mine, Sergeant. Mine's to evaluate the medical evidence, and on the purely medical evidence it's suicide."

He persisted: "Could someone have fed her that stuff?"

"Against her will?" said Tina. "Forced a handful of capsules down her throat? I don't think so, Sergeant. It's almost impossible to do such a thing without leaving clear signs of a struggle on the victim. Extensive defensive bruising. Skin tissue under the fingernails."

Turner nodded. "I expect you're right, Doctor," he said with some reluctance.

"You'll have my written report tomorrow," said Tina.

"Still, we'll chase up that missing two hundred and fifty," he said. "There's some who'd think that no one in his right mind would murder for a measly two hundred and fifty nicker. But we know better, don't we, ma'am?"

"I once did a P.M. on an old woman of seventy who was battered to death for seventy-five pence," said Tina.

"It's a funny world."

They walked out together. Tina had phoned for a mini-cab to take her home, and it was waiting outside. As they parted company, Turner looked rather sheepishly at her and said:

"I wonder if I could have your autograph, Doctor. You're a great favourite with all my relations. Would you mind, please?—it's for my brother's kid."

When she got back to Lochiel Street, Maggie was on the phone to someone at the TV Centre about the rehearsal for the next weekly programme, which generally took place on Monday mornings. At the sight of Tina, she put her hand over the mouthpiece and hissed across to her: "Have you roughed out the cases for next week, he asks."

"Yes," lied Tina, and went to make herself a cup of coffee.

Maggie joined her later in the kitchen.

"Jeremy didn't ring," she informed Tina, "but there was a call from a stranger who wouldn't give his name. I gave him the big brush-off: said you weren't available—just that."

"What did he sound like?" asked Tina.

"A bit louche. Not smooth enough to be trying to sell you life insurance, but quite articulate. One of your many fans, perhaps."

"How would a fan get hold of our new unlisted phone number?"

"If he rings again and you answer it, you'll be able to ask him."

"I think I'll take my coffee up to the study and work on next week's cases for the show. See you later, Maggie."

"I guessed you hadn't done them."

Tina smiled broadly and walked out, with You the cat trotting importantly at her heels.

The format of "The Pathologist" was broadly an extension of one part—the most popular part, as emerged from the market researchers—of Dr. Johnny Kettle's original programme. Upon Johnny's death, Simon Elles had offered Tina a contract for three trial programmes followed by an option for another six. The first showing drew a sensational viewers' response and "The Pathologist" was clearly set to run forever—or for so long as the fickle public was willing to put up with it.

The particular element in Kettle's original programme had that wise, avuncular figure expounding upon famous true cases of the recent past which had a strong legal-medical basis, with a fairly low-key commentator acting as his "feed." It was Simon Elles who had hit upon the idea of breaking free of this rather tight format by venturing into the volatile area where fact blends with fiction so that the join is scarcely visible: hence the carefully phrased blurb which implied on the one hand that the cases were from Tina May's files, while in the same breath making the usual general disclaimer applied to all works of fiction. In place of a feed, Elles injected the tart note of an abrasive interrogator in the shape of the porcine, sneering, and supercilious Jakeman. Tina May, who had once been interviewed on TV by Jakeman in an entirely different format, and who had taken an instant and irremediable dislike to him, was only with difficulty persuaded to accept the idea. As it turned out, she was profoundly grateful to Simon Elles for urging her into it. And so was her bank manager.

So it was that, as in the middle of every week, Tina retired to her study and went through the notebook in which she had from time to time jotted down brief synopses of random cases from her personal experience, cases she had heard about from Johnny Kettle, memories of the innumerable forensic paradigms enshrined in the standard textbooks of the canon. She had settled upon the rough outlines of three suitable puzzlers when the phone rang. You raised his head from her lap and gave a bored yawn. She picked up the receiver.

"Hello?"

"Dr. May, ma'am? Detective Sarn't Turner speaking."

"Hello again, Sergeant," responded Tina, and suffering a sudden pang of conscience, added: "I'm going to start on your report just as soon as I've finished what I'm doing."

"Looking forward to seeing it, ma'am. But that wasn't what I rang about. I thought that you'd be concerned to hear that there's been an interesting development—police-wise—in the Waterhouse death that you attributed to suicide."

"Oh yes?"

"In response to our request locally, a couple of witnesses have turned up. It seems that at about the time of the woman's death—as estimated by the police surgeon who first examined the body—Miss Clarice Waterhouse had a visitor."

"Did she, now?" commented Tina.

"Yes, a courting couple have come forward to say that they were in a darkened car parked a few doors down from Miss Waterhouse's place, and that at the material time they observed a certain party leave her place and make off down the road in the opposite direction. Walking quickly, they said."

"Did they get a good description of this party, Sergeant?"

"As we always say, Doctor, there are no *good* descriptions." He sounded disappointed with her. "All we have is that he appeared to be a heavily built man under six feet tall. And no doubt with that two hundred and fifty pounds in his pocket!"

Tina perceived that he could scarcely keep the note of triumph out of his voice.

TWO

Maggie Wainwright's view of the relationship between Tina May, divorcée, and Jeremy Cook, bachelor and barrister-at-law, was overcoloured by her warm and romantic nature. The truth of it was that they had never enjoyed anything in the nature of carnality; brought together purely in the accidental nature of their jobs, they had liked what they had seen, had become good pals in the first instance, and eventually surrogate brother and sister. To Tina, Jeremy was a friend, a comforter and an occasional shoulder to lean on—though not too often; Jeremy displayed to her a gentle puppy-dog adoration that was quite out of character with his reputation of man-about-town, chaser of debutantes, and hell-raiser at the gambling clubs. He was, incidentally, a very good barrister.

The luncheon date sealed by Maggie in Tina's absence, no further arrangements were required; they simply met "as usual" at twelve forty-five precisely in a favourite pub off Fleet Street. And, true to tradition, Jeremy was there first. There was already a gin and tonic in the place facing him across their usual corner table. He was exactly one third of the way down a pint tankard of best bitter ale.

They kissed and squeezed hands. "What have you been up to?" she asked.

"I've got most resounding news for you, Tina," he replied. "But it will have to wait till the pudding stage. Doing anything exciting? I saw your last show and it was super. But why do you have to put up with that creep Jakeman? Surely by now you've got enough popularity muscle to have him seen off."

"Darling, I've always thought that the Law gives people a blinkered view of life," she responded. "Why else would learned judges require, by some silly old convention, to demand the definition of things like 'rock 'n' roll,' 'Coca-Cola,' 'Star Wars,' and the like?"

He grinned. "It's really a very sound convention, Tina," he said. "You'd be surprised at the number of jurors who're in blissful ignorance of such things. The assumption of judicial ignorance is for their benefit. But you didn't answer my question."

"Toby Jakeman is this, and he is that," said Tina, "but, by some strange alchemy which will always evade you, and I have accepted only with reluctance, he's just about the biggest thing that happened to middle-aged women since Rudolph Valentino. And there are figures to prove it . . . Heavens! Talking of the goggle-box, there's a programme I simply *have* to watch at one!"

Inured as he was to the unexpected vacillations of witnesses hostile and otherwise, Jeremy was quick to respond to the change of tack. Downing his beer in one gulp, he seized her hand.

"No sooner said than done!" he cried. "Come with me!"

Twenty close-up faces in varying degrees of focus and colour; twenty loudspeakers declaiming in unison that this was the "Lunch-Hour Show" presented by David Hobday, and Hobday's face it was that filled the twenty screens laid end to end in the electrical-goods emporium to which Jeremy Cook had conveyed her.

"May I be of assistance?" A suave salesman sidled up, did a double take upon recognising Tina, and backed away obsequiously, as if from the presence of royalty.

"You can see the join in Hobday's wig," said Jeremy.

"Sssh!" from Tina.

Hobday mellifluously introduced an ordinary British housewife whose claim to fame lay in the fact of her having baked and iced a monster cake for the Queen's birthday; this edifice, a replica of Windsor Castle, had been graciously acknowledged by Her Majesty's private secretary. Then followed a new pop group whose sheer awfulness was a certain passport to their success.

And then . . .

"Next, an unusual item," beamed Hobday. "The ancient art of falconry, or hawking, if you prefer it, has had a revival in the post-war years, and a considerable part of this revival can be attributed to my next guest. I present Mr. Jamie Farrell, former seaman, now a full-time falconer, teacher, demonstrator, and practitioner of the art."

The image was switched to Farrell, in close up, with the eyas "Baby" on his gauntleted fist. In sharp contrast to the emollient Hobday, he looked relaxed, even bored; yet there was an inner vitality lying in repose which Tina supposed that she had noticed in him, but was strangely magnified through the medium of TV.

"That's the man I wanted to see, Jeremy," she said. "I'll tell you about him later."

The presenter closed with his subject and addressed himself to the hawk, who, as Tina was not surprised to notice, gathered herself to take wing in alarm.

"Vicious-looking creature," commented Hobday. "That wickedly curved beak! I bet that could give you a nasty wound."

"She wouldn't demean herself," was Farrell's flat response. "She kills with her talons. The beak's simply for tearing the flesh off your bones."

"That's very interesting," said Hobday, and he contrived to look interested. "You mean, if I were to sort of make a grab at her, she'd lunge at me with those horribly sharp claws?"

"Try it and see," said the other.

"And if one were a mouse, a rabbit, or some such—she'd do one considerable damage?"

"If you were a small enough *human being*, or she a big

enough goshawk, she'd crush the life out of you," was the flat response, delivered with no shadow of facial expression.

"Crikey!" exclaimed Jeremy Cook. "That's telling him!"

The rest of the interview was carried out in similar vein: with Hobday manfully struggling to dictate the tenor of the dialogue, but being outpaced, outfaced, outscripted by the implacable man with the hawk. At a suggestion from the visibly unhappy presenter, Farrell demonstrated the technique of flying the half-trained hawk on a length of fine, stout line called a creance, so that she flew at his fist on the word of command, commenting the while—but directly at the camera and totally ignoring the by then largely irrelevant Hobday, who could do no more than nod and beck and occasionally opine that it was all very interesting.

"Well," said Jeremy Cook when it was over, "I must say your friend's very impressive."

"Yes, he is, isn't he?" mused Tina.

"Useful chap to have as a companion in a lifeboat, I should think."

"I think you've got him just about right, Jeremy," she said.

"But I'd be damned glad to be rescued, and rid of his company," added Jeremy.

Their emergence from the electrical-goods emporium was by no means easily accomplished; by the time Jamie Farrell's spot was over, the plate-glass windows were lined with regarding faces agog to see a television personality plain; it called for a lot of autographing to win their way to a taxi which Jeremy seized from out of the scudding lunch-hour traffic to deposit them at the Savoy.

In the subdued murmuring of the grill-room, they talked of cabbages and kings—and the egregious Jamie Farrell—through smoked salmon and *boeuf en croute*.

Finally, addressing herself to her profiteroles, Tina said: "Out with it, darling. You've been dying to unburden yourself from the moment we met. What's this resounding news you can't wait to tell me?"

For answer, Jeremy gave a broad, conspiratorial wink and producing from his pocket (with the air of conjuror producing a rabbit out of a hat) a tiny box, he opened it on the table and revealed within a five-stone diamond ring.

"It's very nice, Jeremy," she said, "but diamonds fade on me."

"Silly idiot!" he said. "I know it would be a waste of time to propose to you—you wouldn't have me if there was a free packet of super detergent thrown in."

"Then who's the lucky girl—or, as I presume—the lucky girl-to-be? Does she know of her imminent luck?"

"She's got a pretty good idea," said Jeremy smugly, "and her name's Jessica Rothstein."

"No relation to? . . ."

"Yes, Tina. Lord Rothstein's her daddy." He spoke the name of arguably the most eminent, prestigious, most publicised and highly paid member of the legal profession: an archsolicitor whose spectrum of influence ran from the confidential advisor of governments to the easing of multimillionare pop stars through grotesque entanglements with the law. Tina had vaguely heard of the daughter Jessica, and mostly in connection with what she compartmented generally in the category of "good works," which in Ms. Rothstein's case included such things as international child welfare, aid to the Third World, various animal interests, penal reform, and so forth.

Another thought also struck Tina; she decided upon the instant to approach it obliquely . . .

"Where did you meet her, Jeremy?" (Surely not at one of the high-toned gambling clubs at which, if the society glossies were to be believed, her surrogate brother passed that part of his life which he kept apart from her.)

"Well, actually, it was more than a year ago at a dinner party at the Strutherses. Lady Miriam—the drunken bitch—was into a big campaign to get herself socially accepted again after her dear old dad's antics had got them excluded from the royal enclosure at Ascot. It was at the time when Rothstein père was practically running the Home Office from his chambers in Pall Mall. I don't know what came of that particular ploy of Lady M.'s, but Jessica sat next to me at dinner and we got on like a house on fire. She was very big, at that time, in a fund-raising thing to relieve famine in Central Africa, and my father, as you know, Tina, was once a High Commissioner out there, so we—um—found we had an awful lot in common. She's awfully nice, Tina. You'll love her."

Tina made no reply.

"She—um—is very artistic. The old boy, you know, he's got the finest collection of Post-Impressionists outside the Tate Gallery and the Louvre. And she's very into music. Vivaldi and all that stuff." He pushed a piece of orange cheesecake around its plate—unenthusiastically. "I think she'll make me a good wife. A settling influence, know what I mean? After all, I'm pushing thirty-five and I can't keep up this man-about-town kick for much longer. *Why don't you say something, Tina?*" he cried. And every head turned to regard them. "I'm sorry," he said, pushing his plate to one side.

"I've never met her," said Tina, "but I would suppose she's a bit older than you?"

"She's forty."

"It's a nice age. She's got her best years in front of her. You say she's got a good idea that you're going to propose to her?"

"Yes, Tina." He grinned ruefully. "If I weren't pretty sure, I wouldn't have got an extension on my overdraft to buy the ring." The grin faded. "If she turns me down, I don't suppose I shall get more than sixty percent on a resale after the mark-up, value added tax, and so forth has been deducted by the guy who flogged it to me!"

"Jeremy—Jeremy . . ." She reached out and laid her hand over his. "Do you really have to do this?"

He was the little boy again, and she the older, wise sister. He bit his lip and avoided her eyes when he replied: "I'm being dunned from every direction," he said. "The tax people, the bank, everywhere—but mostly the tax people, who're threatening me with sequestration if I don't cough up more or less immediately."

"Oh, Jeremy, why didn't you tell me this before?" she asked him. "Thanks to the TV programme, I'm fairly rolling in it at the moment, and I could help you out. How much is involved?"

He told her—and with one eyebrow cocked wryly at her, gauging her reactions and guessing what they would be. The figure he threw at her was quite astronomical.

"Oh!" said Tina.

"Quite," he said. "You see what I mean, darling? It isn't merely a matter of a small loan from a dear chum to tide me over a sticky bit; what I have is an historic debt, a snowball of a debt that I've been pushing ahead of me for years and has grown out of all control. It began when I was first called to the Bar and had a great slice of beginner's luck by being involved in winning a couple or so notorious cases at the Bailey. I took to spending every penny that came in—not putting anything aside for tax. Then old Forbes-Bennett, the guy who was my Leader and in whose long shadow I was riding the gravy train, went and died on me. Then followed a sticky patch where I didn't have a brief for over a year. So I took to keeping body and soul together by the only way that came to hand . . ."

"Gambling," supplied Tina.

"Right first time. Oh, it was no sweat, for gambling's in my blood. My dear old dad lost every penny he had, mortgaged the family estate, lost out with his wife, his career—everything—in pursuit of Lady Luck. Oh yes—young Jeremy took to it like the proverbial duck takes to water. And simply sank even lower."

She regarded him warily, knowing that nothing would ever be the same between them again if she jibbed at what had to be said; yet hideously aware of the consequences if she were to frame her thoughts infelicitously.

"So now you plan to marry your way out of debt, Jeremy—do I have it right?" she asked, opting for the direct approach.

Again that grin—self-mocking, yet curiously heartening. "Right on the nose, as usual, Tina. Yes, darling, that's about the size of it. With any luck, Poppa Rothstein will settle my debts. I shall creep under the warm umbrella of his patronage and receive an endless string of briefs in the prestigious —and highly paid—area of company law and the like. And the rough-and-tumble of the Criminal Bar at the Old Bailey will see me no more."

"I think it's a great pity, Jeremy," she murmured, and hoped he did not see her sudden tears.

On the way back to Lochiel Street, she hardened her heart against sentiment by telling herself that, yes, it *was* unworthy of an honest, straightforward, clever and likeable person such as Jeremy to go fortune-hunting, but given his circumstances, there didn't really seem to be any other way out. But it still hurt her to dwell upon it; furthermore, there was the nagging thought that, given all of Jeremy's virtues as she listed them to herself, he was proving himself to be short on a virtue that she probably prized above all others—and that was basic integrity.

Maggie was out at lunch, still, when she got back, and the telephone rang almost immediately she took off her coat. It was Janet Barden, of Samuel, Smiley, Todd & Arundel—solicitors. Janet had once retained her to keep a watching brief at a rather tricky exhumation on which had stood an issue of possible murder. After that, they had become firm friends, the older woman and the younger, and now that her affairs had become more complicated in the matter of contracts and so forth, Janet had become her own solicitor.

"Tina, we have trouble," was her opening gambit.

"Oh dear, don't say this," responded Tina. "I've only just come back from a horrendous luncheon with a friend who's planning to ruin his life—and someone else's. What's it all about, Janet?"

"I don't want to talk about it over the phone, Tina. Can

you come round to the office this afternoon? I've got a client waiting outside. Can you make it—say—a quarter to four?"

"Sure. But can't you give me some idea of what it's all about, Jan?"

"All I can say is, it's a really dirty business!"

With that, she rang off. Tina charitably assumed that the client had just been ushered in.

She was at Samuel, Smiley, Todd & Arundel's at three forty-five on the dot, and being shown in to Janet Barden's office while the chimes of the quarter hour were still dying over the winter-parched grass of Lincoln's Inn Fields. Janet —widowed, motherly, fortyish, and plump—waved her to a seat. The good-humoured and intelligent eyes were still affectionate as she regarded the younger woman, but Tina was uneasily aware that her friend was wearing her legal hat for the occasion—and remembered that Janet Barden was known as one of the keenest minds in criminal practice, which she handled exclusively for her firm.

"Well, Jan, I can see something's badly wrong. Out with it," said Tina.

The other nodded. "I should like you to bear with me, Tina," she responded. "To cut corners, I'm going to interrogate you and arrive at some answers which will put you right in the picture without a lot of flim-flam. Do you follow me?"

"Perfectly." Despite herself, Tina was amused by her friend's tough line.

"Okay. Hark back to last June. Do you recall performing a post-mortem on Dawn Harkness?"

"The cabinet minister's daughter—yes, I remember it well. She was killed in a car accident. She was with a party of gay young things. The boy driving the car lived to tell the tale, but was imprisoned for drunk driving and manslaughter . . ."

"Never mind about him. We're not concerned with his problems!" Janet's tone was determinedly imperious. "Regarding the P.M.—what were your findings?"

"Why—death from multiple injuries, what else? The girl went straight through the windscreen at about eighty miles an hour. That the driver survived was nothing less than a mira . . ."

"The injuries apart, what of her condition—did you report on that?"

"Yes—negatively. The rest of the party—who were all older than the Harkness girl—had certainly been drinking heavily, probably taking drugs. I don't know. I didn't examine them, but they were a pretty notorious crowd of gilded youth gone to the bad. Dawn Harkness, however, had had no more than the equivalent of two tots of one or another of the common brands of vermouth with tonic water added. And definitely no drugs. She was—several months under sixteen years of age when she was killed."

A brief silence. Janet Barden studied a sheet of typescript that lay on the desk before her. Her next question, when it came, was delivered in a quiet voice and loaded with significance: "What else did you find, Tina?"

Tina drew breath sharply—and exhaled it slowly.

"I found her to be three months pregnant, Jan."

"And did this not figure in your report?"

"No."

"Why? Tell me why!"

"Oh, Jan—come off it! It's pretty obvious why not."

"Speaking as a solicitor—not to me it isn't obvious!"

"All right. I'm retained on a panel of pathologists by the Home Office, and from time to time I'm called upon to perform post-mortems—perfectly routine and straightforward post-mortems—in cases of death through accident. I reported on this case to the effect that the girl—child—died of multiple injuries, that she had been virtually stone cold sober at the time. The fact of her being pregnant was entirely irrelevant. God damn it, Jan—the poor parents had enough grief to bear without the added burden of knowing that their fifteen-year-old kid had got herself in the family way."

"They didn't know she was pregnant, do you suppose?"

"I know they didn't—yes, I'm a hundred percent sure they didn't."

"How can you be so sure?"

"Because I met them socially some months later. I expressed my condolences and was able to assure them that Dawn died instantaneously. If they'd known about her, I'm sure they—Jennifer at least—would have brought it up."

"You call Mrs. Harkness by her given name—are you well acquainted with them, then?"

"Not well," replied Tina. "We met at dinner parties occasionally, but not recently. They were really Johnny Kettle's friends, and he used to take me about, as you know. All right, out with it, Jan," she added. "What *is* all this? I've answered all your questions and you've uncovered my small sin of omission. What next?"

"A few more questions, Tina," replied the other. "Tell me —have you been following the news recently—as it concerns David Harkness, M.P., in particular?"

"Why, yes—hasn't he been proposing a rather strong line with the young unemployed? Implying that they don't even want to work, but much prefer to live on the state. Take drugs. Sleep around all over the place . . . Oh!" she looked across at her friend. "Does something begin to click in my mind, Jan?"

In reply, Janet Barden said: "Do you remember who it was assisted you at the post-mortem on Dawn Harkness, Tina?"

"Ah yes, I do as a matter of fact. One of the full-time attendants at the Borough District Mortuary. A rather shifty individual, but quite efficient. Name of—ah—Skerrit."

"Well, I'm sorry to tell you, Tina, that Skerrit is also party to the knowledge of the dead girl's condition," said Janet Barden, "and I have it on the legal grapevine that he has blown the whole story—your part in it included—to the *Sunday Courier*. And you know what a meal *that* rag will make of it next Sunday!"

Janet's secretary brought them tea and biscuits.

The solicitor had unbent; the friend had re-emerged.

"I have a pirated copy of his story to the *Courier*," she said. "It's so factual that it has to be believed. Apparently, during your examination you said, half to yourself: 'What have we got here?' followed by: 'Oh, you poor kid.' True, Tina?"

Tina nodded. "Just like that," she said. "My very words."

Janet drained her cup and carefully replaced it on the saucer.

"The flavour of the month is 'Cover Up'," she said. "Your friend Skerrit, who as a prominent member of one of the more way-out revolutionary parties and just about as diametrically opposite David Harkness in the political spectrum as it is possible to be, put that poor girl's pathetic secret in the back of his molelike mind against the right occasion cropping up. Harkness's diatribe against the indigent young is tailor-made for him.

"The *Courier* will run it as a cover-up engineered by you to protect the good name of the girl's family, with your friend Harkness's approval. They'll cut him to ribbons—but that isn't my worry: politicians who open their big mouths too wide and too often have to learn to take the rough with the smooth. And they frequently learn very quickly. I'm more worried about you, dear, and your professional reputation once this is splashed all over that scandal rag. Do you follow me?"

Tina followed her, all right.

Dr. Tina May's report, filed along with an appreciation by Detective Sergeant Turner of the Waterhouse case, was on the desk of Detective Chief Inspector Derek Arkwright in New Scotland Yard by noon, and he had minuted the file and put it into the Out tray for the Deputy Commissioner when Turner knocked and came in.

"Sir, we've had a call from Croydon. Another bride-in-the-bath-style case. Only this time it's a male—retired greengrocer named Foy. Sixty-one. Widower. I checked it out straightaway—he withdrew over a thousand pounds from his bank yesterday and a first search by the local boys hasn't revealed a trace of it in the house."

"In the bath, you say—has the body been shifted?"

"Not yet, sir. I told them to leave everything where it was."

Arkwright got to his feet and called his secretary through the office door; she came running.

"Joyce, get on to Dr. May. Ask her will she please join us immediately at an address in Croydon. Tell her it might be another of Detective Sergeant Turner's famous brides-in-the-bath affairs, and that I'm sending a car round for her right away.

"Come on, Turner. Get your coat and let's go."

A fast patrol car and two motorcycle outriders drove the two men down to Croydon. They went in silence: Arkwright had brought along his briefcase with a load of what he called his "homework"; Turner concentrated upon what he hoped and believed was the flowering of *the* significant case of his career, one which would raise him up as he wished to be raised, and establish the "new boy" from Criminal Records as a detective to be reckoned with. *If only Dr. Tina doesn't muddy the stream,* he thought.

They came to a road lying just off the main high street of Croydon, in an Edwardian enclave that had had its ups and downs since World War I and was now fairly established in the era where demolish it and build a glass-and-concrete monstrosity had given way to conserving what remained and at considerable cost. The district was solid bourgeois and Arkwright counted some quite prestigious cars parked outside the heavily tarted-up semi-detached villas with their venetian blinds and their cream front doors, and even one Rolls-Royce—albeit past its prime.

Three patrol cars, a command car and several police motorcycles were huddled in front of a house on the far corner of the street. The crackle of static from the command car greeted them as they alighted, and a uniformed sergeant saluted Arkwright. There was the usual gaggle of rubberneckers, but the local constabulary had set up crush barriers.

Arkwright was greeted by the officer in charge, a youngish uniformed inspector whom he knew by sight.

"We got straight in touch with you, at the Yard, Mr. Arkwright," he said, "having received the circular regarding this drowning-in-the-bath case in Tooting the other day. Apart from the fact that the victim's a man, there appear to be several parallels."

"Lead the way," said Arkwright.

The bathroom was on the second floor back of the substantial, semi-detached Edwardian house. It was in an additional wing that had been built out at the rear in an early stage of modernisation some time between the wars to accommodate bathroom, kitchen, and lavatory. Glazed on three sides with the leaded lights of the period, it was a cross between a greenhouse and a temple to Art Nouveau. Despite the chill of the wintry day, it struck warm in the room; there was a radiant heater burning on the wall opposite the bath.

In the bath, face all but submerged save for nose and nostrils and a fuzz of grey moustache, was the nude body of a man in late middle age. The eyes were open; they stared—fishlike under the water—up at the ceiling.

A police surgeon was packing his instruments back into his bag. "Difficult to ascertain time of death," he said. "The water is almost tepid now, but it helped retain the body heat for a considerable while, of course. And the room temperature's fairly high, so I'd say that heater's been on since last night. That conforms with my view that he died last night, some time between, say eight o'clock and midnight. Is the body to be moved straightaway?"

Arkwright told him that the eminent pathologist Dr. May was coming, information which he greeted with a shrug and a muttered comment about *force majeure.* Then he left.

Footsteps on the stairs a quarter of an hour later issued in Tina and her escorts. As always when he met her, Derek Arkwright experienced that special kind of delight which encouraged him, a bachelor in his late forties, in the hope of finding "that not impossible she" before it was too late.

"Tina, thanks for coming," he said, taking her hand.

"Hello, Derek. How are you?"

They had known and liked each other since working together on the notorious "Green-eyed Woman Case" which was Tina's introduction to a certain fame.* Now an accredited consultant to New Scotland Yard, she met him quite frequently—and usually, as on this occasion, in the presence of a corpse.

"What we have so far, Tina," said Arkwright, "is that he died some time between eight and midnight last night. What do you want to do now—shall we have him lifted out?"

"I think so, Derek," she said. "There's not much one can do under water. If you'd lay him out here on the rug, I'll take the body temperature and see if there are any marks that don't show in the present position. After that, we'd better have him over at the mortuary for a P.M."

Two stalwart constables lifted out the corpse of the retired greengrocer and laid it reverently on the floor beside the bath. Tina knelt beside the body and got to work.

"Yes, I'd go along with the estimate as to time of death," she said presently. "Sooner earlier than later. Eight o'clock would be about right. Cause of death—as in the other case— quite clearly asphyxia by drowning. Whether there are any contributory causes remains to be seen." She was examining the pallid skin of the body, beginning at the feet and ankles and working up to the hands, arms, the chest, the neck . . .

"There's a bruise here!" she exclaimed. "See, Derek? Just under the right ear. I would say it's a thumb mark."

"A thumb mark for sure," confirmed Arkwright. "And applied with some considerable force, wouldn't you say?"

"Oh yes. And before death."

Tina looked up at him, and at the row of faces regarding her, Turner's included. "So what we have," she said, "is

* *No Escape*, by Sarah Kemp (Doubleday, 1984).

nothing at all like the Waterhouse case, which could quite easily have been what it appeared to be—a straight suicide. Here, there is every indication that the victim was brutally grabbed by the throat and held under till he drowned."

"But he must have struggled—kicked out—when he was being held under!" interjected Turner. "The floor should be swimming with water, but it's bone dry. The heat of the room couldn't account for that!"

Tina rose to her feet. "Let's move the body over to the mortuary," she suggested.

Turner and Arkwright stood aside to let her go out of the door. On the way, she paused and pointed to a towel rail set against the wall.

"That's odd," she said. "A bathroom—but no bath towel."

"I've got it!" exclaimed Turner. "The killer mopped up the water from the floor with the bath towel. But where is it now, this sodden towel?"

"He took it with him," supplied Tina May. "Dead men don't get out of the bath and mop up their mess. And the killer wants us to think it's suicide."

THREE

After a nerve-racking, tearing-about kind of day, Tina was glad to get back to Lochiel Street, to the warmth of her fireside, the company of Maggie Wainwright, her feet up on the sofa, tea and hot buttered crumpets.

A letter had arrived for her on the second post. It was undated and bore no letterhead:

Dear Dr May,

I rang you several times, but you were either not in or there was no reply. I wonder if you would care to have lunch with me? If so, would you meet me at the Endive Restaurant in Edgeware Road on Friday at 1 P.M.

If you don't turn up, I shall quite understand. I am not everyone's choice of a lunch companion.

Yours sincerely,
Jamie Farrell

"How very odd," she said, and passed the letter over to Maggie, who read it.

"Is this the nut you told me about?" she asked. "The guy with the golden eagle, or whatever?"

"That's him, Maggie. But the curious thing is that, although he's an absolute conversation-stopper in real life and the sort one wouldn't choose to take one's last lunch on earth with, he comes over quite remarkably strongly on TV. Even Jeremy was impressed."

"He must be the phantom caller who wouldn't give his name."

"Yes, that would be quite in character for him."

"Shall you keep the date, Tina?"

Tina tapped the letter against her chin. "I don't know. Friday's two whole days away. I'll keep my options open. At least, I don't have a return address or phone number, so he's got no beef if, upon mature reflection, I find that I have a prior engagement."

Maggie frowned and shook her head. "Don't get entangled with a nut-case like him, Tina," she admonished. "I've heard quite enough about Jock your first. You would seem to have a taste for eccentrics. The last thing we want around this place is birds of prey flying out in one's face every time one opens a cupboard door."

Tina laughed and nearly choked on a mouthful of crumpet.

"Idiot!" she said. "As if I would!"

"Seriously, you look worried sick, duckie," said Maggie. "Are you brooding about this Dawn Harkness business?"

"Yes, I am," admitted Tina. "I've had trouble with the *Sunday Courier* before, and they really are a dirty lot. I don't know what to do about it. I quizzed Jan Barden as to whether I should contact David Harkness and alert him if he didn't already know, but she told me to keep my head down and leave it to her."

"How did the panic call to Croydon go?"

"Well, I have to say that perked me up a lot and got the old adrenaline moving. There might really be a murder case in this. The chap who died—or more likely was killed in his bath—yielded up some very interesting facts at the P.M."

"Yes?" Maggie poured them both another cup of tea.

"He was very heavily into Valium. We checked with his local doctor, who said he'd prescribed it for depression. That much I found inside him—but also what must have been the biggest part of half a bottle of whisky. His killer, before following him into the bathroom and drowning him, must have deliberately rendered him half blotto with booze."

Maggie Wainwright shuddered. All of a sudden it seemed

to her that their cosy fireside companionship was very fragile —and that the big tom-cat on Tina's lap, who stirred, stretched himself and yawned, his incisors bared and his talons extended, was a symbol of the jungle that lay all around them—even in the quiet streets of Chelsea.

The following day passed quite uneventfully, with Tina putting in several hours on a book which had at present only a tentative title: a treatise on violent crime that she had been working on with Johnny Kettle up to the time of his death. It was a difficult and demanding subject that called for a lot of research. Tina, who was essentially a clinician rather than an academic (as indeed, so had been Kettle, or the book would have been further advanced than it was!), found the attendant research time-consuming and tedious. But it had the advantage of taking herself out of herself, and a change of pace.

She reminded herself, by checking with her diary, that she had acknowledged the receipt of an invitation, and agreed to go that evening, to a private view of pictures by a young artist named Clive Lorant, one of whose delicate landscapes she had bought at the previous year's Royal Academy Summer Exhibition. It seemed as good a way as any to wind up the day, and it gave her an opportunity to wear one of the rather extravagant Spring outfits that her new-found affluence had made possible.

At six-thirty, bathed and dressed, she phoned for a cab and was driven to Bond Street in a flurry of snow, past newsstands where the placards read:

MURDER VICTIM FOUND IN HARROW!

News-wise, it had been a dull week: the strange demise of the Croydon greengrocer had been kept under wraps by the police as a matter of policy. The murder in question, at Harrow, won itself a mere five-inch single column at the foot of the front page, and only featured on the placards as a catch-penny:

HARROW WIDOW MURDERED

The anxious enquiries of her elder sister,
who had expected to see her last Friday,
led local police to the house of Mrs Alice
Pouter, 58, a widow of The Hollies, Laburnum Drive, Harrow. Upon breaking in,
they found Mrs Pouter dead in her
kitchen, where she had been brutally murdered. A considerable sum of money
which the dead woman had planned to
take with her to her sister's had been
stolen from her ransacked suitcase. Police
enquiries continue.

Displaying no connection with the drownings-in-the-bath
syndrome, the *modus operandi* of the killing had allowed it to
slip unchallenged through the computers at New Scotland
Yard—as the manner of the newspaper presentation suggested to the killer whom the dead woman had known as
Norman.

Norman sat in a café off Piccadilly, not five hundred yards
from the elegant Bond Street picture gallery where the taxi
delivered Tina May. He sat sipping tea and dunking fingers
of toast into that oversweetened brew, the newspaper
propped up in front of him at the lower half of the front
page, and he nodded and grinned at the relevant paragraph.

The Pinxit Gallery, brain-child of Hugo and Petronella
Delouthe, had been opened only a short while, but that
eminent couple, through their admirable connections socially and in the media, had built up a solid following for
their small but excellent stable of painters, engravers, and
sculptors.

The place was crowded when Tina entered. She was immediately importuned to accept a champagne cocktail, spotted by the watchful Petronella and led into the throng.

"My dears, I don't have to introduce my star of the evening—Dr. Tina!"

"Oh, you're so much more beautiful than you appear on the box!"

"I can scarcely believe I've seen you in the flesh—you are *you*, aren't you?"

Petronella gently guided her through the brittle throng. "I want you to meet someone else very special, darling," she said, and brought her to a tall figure in legal-clerical grey who turned, on sensing their proximity.

"Why, hello, Tina!"

"Hello, Marc."

"Oh, you two already know each other—I'd quite forgot," said Petronella. "Well, I'll leave you together. Don't get up to any mischief." She winked naughtily and left them. It was her style to spread a little consternation where she trod.

Marcus Struthers, Q.C., held Tina's hand a little longer than convention dictated and treated her to the full benefit of his deep grey gaze. As ever, she experienced in herself a nagging imp of mistrust of this almost absurdly attractive man. He was just a tiny bit too good to be true, she thought. The glance too open and frank, even the slicks of grey over the ears and at the temples were too much the caricature of the handsome man of distinction. And yet—she liked him, for he had never given her the slightest reason to do other.

For his part, Struthers, notwithstanding his assurance, seldom felt at ease with Tina. The product of a back-street slum in Portsmouth, he had won his way, by scholarships and patronage, to the highest echelons of the Bar. A knighthood and high political office lay well within his extended grasp. A marriage to Lady Miriam, daughter of the dissolute Earl of Wycherley, had not been the social lift that he might have anticipated, and he and his wife (the same "drunken bitch" to whom Jeremy Cook had so ungallantly alluded) were supposed to have been divorced long since, leaving him free to make a fresh match with the kind of woman—he fantasized about her frequently—who would grace the role of Lady

Struthers, consort of the Lord High Chancellor of England. He was aware that as often as not it was Tina May whom he clad in the rich apparel of that role, but in spite of that—or perhaps because of it—he always felt at a loss in her presence; setting her on a pedestal on high: chaste, untouchable, Aphrodite descended from Parnassus.

"Greatly admire your TV show, Tina," he said. "How are you enjoying your fame?"

Again that question! . . .

She gave him her stock reply and asked him what he had been doing recently.

"As you may or may not have heard," he said, "Mirrie has at last agreed to collaborate in the divorce. Poor dear, she's had a tremendous amount of hassle with her father, who has been in trouble again with the police. However, Mirrie's found herself a nice, steady boyfriend and I hope he'll make an honest woman of her and they'll settle down in tranquil domesticity. She deserves it. I was just about the last chap on earth she should have married."

And that, thought Tina, is Marc Struthers all over: generous to a fault in his summation of character and situation. She—Tina—who had been present on at least one occasion when Lady Miriam had displayed herself as more like the character so ungallantly depicted by Jeremy Cook, knew how generous Marc had been. He really was quite a nice guy.

"And so," said Struthers, "by way of a celebration, I'm off to beautiful Ravello just as soon as the Hilary Law Term's finished next week. Do you know Ravello, Tina? It overlooks the Gulf of Salerno. There's a hotel on the heights—it used to be the summer villa of the Archbishop of Naples. In the evening, the fishermen bring their catches up the winding road and sell them in the square in front of the church. You'll love Ravello . . . Hey!" he exclaimed, suddenly emboldened. "Why don't you come with me, Tina? No strings attached, of course," he added—somewhat less boldly.

Not taking him at all seriously (and Struthers was quite serious), Tina laughed it off.

"La, sir," she said, in the manner of the standard heroine of the classic-style barnstorming melodrama when addressing the suave villain, "you do have a smooth tongue and a way of turning the head of a simple country gel!"

Next day he sent her flowers, and she had an inkling that he might have been serious after all.

Following upon certain enquiries among the neighbours, the police elicited that Miss Clarice Waterhouse, a spinster with no known relations, had shortly before her murder been an infrequent attender at the Gravely Road Spiritualist Church, and furthermore that, according to various members of the congregation, she had struck up an acquaintance, if not a friendship, with a certain Miss Slyte, a retired infant school headmistress.

In a case where the most ephemeral of leads needs to be treated with the utmost seriousness—and New Scotland Yard had determined that this was just such a case—only the top brass are allowed to tangle with possible material witnesses; so it was that no less than Arkwright and his assistant Turner descended upon the ex-headmistress at her house in Tooting. By appointment.

Miss Slyte was short, stocky, grey-haired, and merry-eyed. She wore a tweed suit, woollen stockings, sensible shoes, and owned an elderly pug dog who slept on her lap throughout the interview, which she had enlivened, for the benefit of the two detectives, with coffee and biscuits.

"I found Miss Waterhouse a very sad person," she said, in answer to Arkwright's lead question. "I don't know who introduced her to Gravely Road—it certainly wasn't I—and I'm quite sure that on the few occasions she went she was never convinced. I hasten to add, Mr. Arkwright, that I am not a convinced Spiritualist, but I've derived a certain comfort from my attendances there."

"And surely she must have derived some benefit also," suggested Arkwright, "for in the last few weeks of her life she never went out of the house—apart from going down to the shops—save to the Spiritualist Church. What do you think, Miss Slyte?"

His implied deference to her opinion as a professional and a *cognosciente* struck the right note with the former headmistress, for she visibly preened herself before replying:

"Mr. Arkwright. As I have said, Miss Waterhouse was a very sad person," she declared. "Early on, she confided in me that she had been attracted to spiritualism for the sole purpose of renewing contact with her mother—I may say, since it was the term she used always—her 'beloved mother.' "

"Ah!" exclaimed Arkwright. "And for what purpose, Miss Slyte?"

The elderly woman spread her pink, plump hands. "That is a very shrewd question," she said. "And I will answer it as well as I am able. Miss Waterhouse, as I learned from my relatively brief acquaintance with her, had spent the larger part of her adult life as companion and nurse to her invalid mother, who was totally incapable of attending to herself, with everything that implies. Nevertheless, Mrs. Waterhouse, even in her supine condition, was able to exercise a most remarkable ascendancy over the only offspring of her marriage—the husband, so I believe, was killed in the war.

"When the mother died, so my conversations with Miss Waterhouse led me to suppose, the daughter was totally bereft of all support, and became—if the simile is not too farfetched—like a ship without a sail. Instinctively, the poor creature turned back to the helpless invalid who, though helpless, had exercised from her bed and her wheelchair all the real guidance that she had ever known."

"What guidance was she seeking, in particular, Miss Slyte?" asked Arkwright.

"Ah, that you must elicit for yourself, Mr. Arkwright," said the ex-headmistress, and wagged a finger at him. "I do not claim the privilege of the confessional, but there are matters —as I think you will appreciate—which are sacred as between one civilised person and another."

Turner made as if to interject an indignant remark; Arkwright stifled it at birth with a withering glance.

"I respect your confidence, Miss Slyte," he said, rising. "And thanks for your help. You've cleared my mind on certain aspects of this case, and I shall probably come and see you again—when I've determined what it was that directed Miss Waterhouse to seek advice from her dead mother."

On that inconclusive note, the interview—interrogation—ended.

Friday came, with it a run-through of the recordings of the next two "Pathologist" shows, which Tina watched with the top brass in the plush projection room at the TV studio. With nothing else on offer and a free afternoon, her footsteps directed her towards the Edgware Road and a restaurant called the Endive, which her cab driver had some difficulty in locating.

It was a modest but nicely appointed place. A pleasant Chinese girl checked in her coat and briefcase.

"I'm Mr. Farrell's guest," she explained.

"Ah, Mr. Farrell is here and awaiting you, madam," said the girl. "Please to come this way, Dr. May."

Farrell was waiting for her at a table in the far corner of an L-shaped dining room which was about half filled with the sort of people whom Tina loosely docketed as "academics": that is to say the menfolk were largely bearded and unfashionably long-haired, the women dressed in a manner that used to be called "bluestocking." There was a proliferation of granny-glasses.

Her host rose upon her arrival and vigorously shook her proffered hand.

"I thought your TV spot was great," she said in all sincerity, by way of breaking the ice, which, she immediately discerned, was rather thick.

He beamed shyly and was obviously pleased. "If it hadn't been for that Hobday merchant getting in the way, I might have struck a blow for British falconry as we know it," he said.

"I'm sure you would," Tina assured him. "Even with him on your back, you did pretty well. I'm inclined to try a hand at it myself," she added. "Falconry, I mean."

"It's by no means an exclusively male sport," said Farrell. "In fact it was greatly favoured by the feminine upper crust in medieval and Tudor times—and later. To someone like you, who enjoys a challenge, it might be a most stimulating experience. "By the way, I'm sorry I was a bit rough with you the other day," he added. "And this meal's by way of being a sort of restitution."

"Thanks, I appreciate that," she responded, and guessed that the gesture had not come to him easily.

The dialogue languished a little . . .

"Whatever induced you to become a forensic pathologist?" he asked out of the blue. "I suppose I've got the term right?"

"Quite right," replied Tina. "Forensic scientists are the folks who apply ballistic principles to spent cartridges and compare microscopic slivers of material to establish a presence at the scene of a crime. We pathologists deal in dead bodies. There was a move afoot in the press, when I had achieved a certain nascent fame, to dub me 'The Corpse Doctor'; thank God the basic decency of the great British public rejected it."

Menus were brought by an obsequious maître-d'. Tina, upon a few moments appraisal of the text, discerned that her host had inveigled her to some kind of vegetarian restaurant of ethnically oriental but demonstrably expensive persuasion. She, whose first love of her young life had been exorcised over nut cutlets and the like in a similar but more modest establishment in Cambridge, deferred to her host in the matter of choosing their fare.

"So what got you into this business?" persisted Farrell, when he had ordered for them both. "Why corpses—why didn't you settle for dealing with the curing of living people?"

It was an old pitch, and she had grown used to delivering it: in the telling, however, it never lost any of its truth for her: "My first idea," she said patiently, "was to be a paediatrician. It didn't work out. I found I didn't have the vocation to watch over little children dying of meningitis and the like. Then I went to a lecture given by Johnny Kettle, and I saw my way through to a career where I didn't have to get involved in life and death; where that issue had already been resolved, and all I had to do was to make my observations as a scientist, write them down in honesty, and feel that I had done my best for the deceased."

"Isn't that a bit of a cop-out?" he asked, looking rather disappointedly at her.

"You may think so," replied Tina coolly. "And you may be right. But it works—for me."

"Put it this way," he said. "You are a trained physician, or surgeon, or whatever—and yet you renege on the very principle of life and death to which you committed yourself when you first took up the racket. What you say is: 'The hell with the whole processes of putting folks right—all I'm interested in is the dead body. Bring me the dead body and I'll tell you what—or who—killed the guy.' Do I have it right?"

"More or less," she replied.

"It's a pretty sterile slant on your profession, isn't it?"

"I don't happen to think so."

He shifted in his chair, displaying every sign of impatience. This he was not able to express for a few minutes whilst they were being served with some kind of very appetising soup. But he soon returned to the attack:

"What do you do, then, if in the normal course of your daily life, you come across a traffic accident where some guy's dying there in the roadway; or you're at a theatre and the manager comes out on stage and calls out in the classic manner is there a doctor in the house?"

"Why, in both cases, I render what aid I can," replied Tina.

"And then?"

"Well, then someone else takes over," she said. "An ambulance arrives, along with a hospital doctor. The person concerned is whisked away to whatever life-support systems are indicated, in the finest possible hospital with the very latest technology."

"Or the guy in question dies right there under your hands."

"Or—as you say—he dies under my hands."

"And that's the part you edge away from."

"The process of dying—yes. I had a friend at university who was doing his pre-medical with me. He suffered from the same thing. After qualifying brilliantly, he switched to dentistry because, as he said, people don't die of teeth."

The meal dragged on with the argument unresolved. Tina, mindful of the impression that Farrell had made upon Jeremy Cook and her in his TV spot, told herself that his uncompromising plain speaking was something one simply had to put up with: a package deal of the whole man, parts of whom were undoubtedly quite interesting and rewarding.

It was only towards the end of the meal that he switched tack: "What's this about your wanting to take up falconry, then?" he asked.

"Seeing you in rapport with that half-trained hawk gave me the inspiration," she said. "I don't suppose it would survive the reality of the thing. It's rather like when I saw a group of people hang-gliding in the Bavarian alps, soaring high above the towers of Schloss Neuschwanstein, and it came to me that this must be the most marvellous experience in life. But to begin with, one would have to face the frightening day when one was expected to jump for the first time off a fairly low hill—and one was scared silly. I rationalised it that way—and forgot it."

"Well," he said, "you'd better come along and see the hawks in action. Are you free any day next week?"

They made a provisional arrangement for her to visit his falconry farm the following Friday.

Tina May was not numbered amongst the millions of her fellow Britons whose Sabbath days were enlivened by the arrival of the *Sunday Courier* on the door mat, to colour the life with scandal, mild pornography, the Royal Family, and cuddly animals in fairly equal proportions.

She had, however, a good relationship with her newsagent and was fairly convinced that when he spotted her name among the contents that Sunday he would slip a copy in through the letter box along with the more prestigious journal of her choice. And so it was.

Janet Barden had not been far wrong in her prediction: the front-page headlines told it all:

"COME OFF IT, HARKNESS!"

says the Sunday Courier.

SCANDALOUS COVER-UP BY "CORPSE DOCTOR"
FAILS TO CONCEAL MINISTER'S HYPOCRISY—

See centre pages.

The centre spread showed pictures of David Harkness, M.P., "and his attractive wife Jennifer, daughter of multimillionaire industrialist Sir Arthur MaGinnis and former debutante of the year." There was a shot of the tragic little Dawn Harkness, taken in her school uniform. And a stock photo of "the Corpse Doctor," Tina May ("combines beauty with a sheer professionalism that makes most TV talking heads look like amateurs").

And there was—the story . . .

It was angled on David Harkness's (admitted, even, by his own party) wildly tactless, more or less off-the-cuff remark at a constituency dinner to the effect that the unemployed young were living off the state in idleness, drug-taking, and promiscuity. Harkness had withdrawn the remarks, the Prime Minister had disassociated the Cabinet and the Government from the remarks—but they had stuck.

POOR LITTLE RICH GIRL . . .

The approach to the dead girl was sheer TV soap opera and a cunning amalgam of schmaltz and censoriousness: on the one hand Dawn had been "the innocent victim of pampered privilege"; on the other "a typical product of the gilded youth whom her father had chosen to ignore when he made his swingeing statement about the underprivileged."
HER SECRET TRAGICALLY REVEALED . . .
The story of the so-called "cover-up" must have cost the *Courier*'s libel lawyers some sleepless nights of vetting and balancing, rephrasing, chopping, and changing. It neither implied nor denied that David Harkness had been a party to suppressing the fact of his daughter's condition; it handed the reader a do-it-yourself plotting kit and invited him to piece it together the way he liked it best. But one fact was made quite plain: Tina May had made the discovery during the post-mortem—and had not included it in her report. And she socialised with the Harknesses.

On Monday morning, Tina received a telegram from her ex-husband:

> DR MAY 18 LOCHIEL STREET LONDON SW
> SUDAN DEAL THROUGHFALLEN DUE POLITICS
> STOP RETURNING BRITAIN STOP HOPING
> YOULL ACCOMMODATE ME TEMPORARILY JOCK

With scarcely time to recover from that shock, there came on Tuesday a letter which sent her flying to the phone, to speak to Janet Barden, who had already spent the biggest part of Sunday afternoon comforting her over the *Courier* article.
"Jan . . ."
"What now, Tina?"
"I've had this letter from the medical council."
"Oh no . . ."
"It's most tactfully put—kindly, indeed. It says that, whilst there's no suggestion that I've been guilty of serious profes-

sional misconduct, the facts revealed in a certain newspaper article suggest that I may have been guilty of *suppressio veri*—which I take to be legalese for the suppression of truth."

"Yes—and? . . ."

"They've set a date for a preliminary proceeding next month, and suggest that I should have myself legally represented. What do I do, Jan?"

"Acknowledge the receipt of the letter and then leave the rest to me, Tina. One of my partners—Dickie Moore—has dealt with the medical council many times, and he'll look after you. But whatever you do—don't worry. A straightforward sin of omission is a hell of a long way from deliberate *suppressio veri*, as we shall demonstrate."

"That horrible, grubby newspaper . . ."

"Yes, I know. It's frightful for you. Look—why don't you get away from it all for a week or so? You've been working much too hard recently—what with your practice and the TV show thrown in."

"I might think about it, Jan—if only to avoid my ex—who's on his way home from the Sudan and threatens to establish himself back in Lochiel Street temporarily—which, like last time, means for the forseeable future."

"Oh, you poor dear. What a rotten run of bad luck you're having. Still—one consolation—everything's bound to be better from now on . . ."

Alas for things getting better!

Tina had a particularly gruelling Tuesday, with two post-mortems in the forenoon, a long and difficult report to write up, and a conference with the programmers of "The Pathologist" in the afternoon which went on till six. She returned to Lochiel Street to find Maggie Wainwright in tears. You the cat had been run over—killed.

Together, they buried him by the wall in the corner of the garden where he had used to sit out and preen himself on sunny days. Supper together in the big kitchen without You imposing his tyrannical will upon events had no flavour for either of them, and Maggie excused herself early and went up to bed.

Around about ten o'clock, Tina had a phone call from Marcus Struthers. After some preliminary condolences about the appalling *Sunday Courier* business, he came out with the real reason for his call, which was to repeat his invitation to accompany him to Ravello.

Something to her surprise, Tina found herself accepting.

FOUR

On the morning of Tina May's flight to Naples with Marcus Struthers (in view of her fame and recent notoriety, they travelled tourist class and she was unrecognised in dark glasses), the killer called Norman breakfasted in some style —mixed grill of sausages, two eggs, bacon, mushrooms and tomatoes, sautéed potatoes, with toast and coffee ad lib—at a popular hotel in the Strand. He ate with a copy of the *Daily Telegraph* propped up against a ketchup bottle before him, and every so often paused in his ingestation to draw a pencilled ring around an item or other in the Deaths, in Memoriam columns. By the end of the meal he had half-a-dozen such. Lingering over his fifth cup of coffee, the killer picked his teeth with a matchstick and, after some consideration, winnowed down his selection to one entry which read as follows:

> VALLENCE.—In loving memory of my dearest husband Major George Edward Vallence, M.C., The Loyal Regiment, of 13, Parkway Close, Finchley, who passed away after a long illness bravely borne a year ago today. From his adoring wife, Teresa. "The long night passeth so slowly, till I shall be with thee once more, Beloved mine."

In no great hurry, he then strolled out to the reception hall, bought himself a red carnation from a pretty salesgirl at the flower kiosk, and had her give him a pound's worth of ten-pence pieces; next, repairing to a vacant phone booth, he riffled through the relevant telephone directory till he found the entry related to Vallence, Maj. G.E., 13 Parkway Close, Finchley—followed by the number.

He dialled—and the number rang out at the other end.

"Hello—yes?"

"Is that Mrs. Vallence?"

"Yes. Who's that, please?"

"Ma'am, you won't know me, but I was in the Loyals with the major. And I was looking through the paper this morning, and I saw . . ." He allowed his voice to break off with the note of a brave man whose eyes are misting treacherously, whose throat has gone unaccountably dry.

"Oh, the In Memoriam! Yes, it was just a year ago that the major was taken, and I miss him so. But I didn't catch your name, Mr.? . . ."

"Wake, ma'am. Formerly Sergeant Wake of the Loyals, who had the honour—and indeed the pleasure—of serving under your husband. And I wondered, since today's the anniversary of the major's passing, I might lay a modest floral tribute on his grave—if you were to direct me to the cemetery in question, ma'am."

"Oh, Mr. Wake, that is so kind, so touchingly kind, of you. Look—why don't you come over and see me this morning? I can show you the major's photo albums. It's highly likely that you are pictured in there somewhere. Oddly, I don't seem to recall your name. Was it in Aden that you were with my husband?"

"Aden—that's right, ma'am."

"Ah well, you see, I didn't accompany him to Aden when the troubles were on there, so that explains why your name's unfamiliar to me. But—look—come straight over, do. We'll talk about old times, look at some photos, and then go over to the crematorium. And lay our floral tributes in the Garden of Remembrance. Yes?"

"Right you are, ma'am."

"See you then, Mr. Wake. You have the address?"

"Yes, ma'am. I'll be over right away."

He came out of the phone booth with the feeling that he would have liked to do a little jig right across the hotel foyer.

"You're in again, mate!" he told himself aloud. "And this one's going to be like taking candy from a baby—just you see if it ain't!"

The drive from Naples airport to the rugged fastness of Ravello—which stands on the heights of the Salerno peninsula between Amalfi and the isle of Capri, facing eastwards across the illimitable blueness of the gulf—they took in a taxi driven by a hot-eyed youth who must have learned his trade in stock-car racing. Presently, by great good fortune, they toiled up the last incline, beneath the overhanging pines and sentinel cypresses, past burgeoning vineyards where cicadas shrilled, to an open square, the mouldering Baroque façade of a church, and a noble archway leading down a cool green-shaded drive to a veritable palazzo.

"The hotel," said Struthers. "And just you wait till you see the view from the terrace."

"Italy, I scarcely know," said Tina. "Save for Venice, where I came a few years ago to a pathologists' conference in January. It was unbearably cold and rained all the time. I have to say, Marc, that everything I've seen since we landed has changed my outlook on Italy entirely."

It was going to be all right, she told herself. The balance of this quite unexpected turn in their relationship had remained quite stable all the way from Heathrow, where he had bought her a glossy magazine and the *Daily Telegraph;* had been quietly attentive to her needs without being pushy. No hand-holding, no assumption of intimacies which they had certainly never shared before. In himself, moreover, he had assumed a mantle of casualness that was markedly at variance with the legal-clerical grey, the bowler hat, the rolled umbrella and briefcase of the distinguished Queen's Counsel; instead, he was in well-cut Black Watch tartan trews, a navy blue sweater, and check sports shirt. They sat together amidst the happy, laughing tourist class and passed muster as a pair of them: no one recognised the fascinating Dr. Tina, the "Corpse Doctor" (hated term!), behind her dark shades. And the tourist classes are not into distinguished Q.C.s, in or out of legal-clerical grey.

The palatial hotel was a sheer delight. They had fairly proximate rooms on the upper floor of the sprawling, sumptuously façaded building, and were able to meet by the simple process of exiting from french windows that issued onto the long balcony which stretched the entire seaward length of the palace. The view over the gulf was breathtaking.

They met there in the late afternoon, when both had unpacked, rested and bathed. Upon Struthers's order, a young waiter brought up a pair of perfect dry martinis, with the instructions to repeat the dose in a quarter of an hour.

They sat together on a swing sofa and sipped their martinis.

"You've heard about Jeremy?" he asked.

"And the Rothstein lady? Yes. He confided in me, and in you also I suppose, Marc. What do you think of it all?"

"Mmm. Well, Tina, I have to say that I don't see any way out for Jeremy save the one he's decided to take. He's a very good barrister, you know, and well liked, with an excellent income. But he simply can't catch up with his historic debt, which largely stems from unpaid tax and his gambling. There's no advancement for him. If he took silk and became a Q.C. he'd immediately lose the steady and lucrative income he earns as a junior. It might take a year—or a lot more to catch up. It's a gamble. And if he moved to the judiciary, he'd be bankrupt in six months. No, I'm afraid poor Jeremy's stuck with little Miss Rothstein—if she'll have him."

"Poor Jeremy," she repeated. "And poor little Miss Rothstein."

"Enough of other people's problems, Tina," he said, "what about yours?"

On the way over, she had told him of the triple disasters: the medical council, Jock's imminent return, the death of the cat You. If it had occurred to Struthers that her ready acceptance of his invitation at the second attempt had been due to this train of misfortunes, he had tactfully given no sign.

"What about this business of *suppressio veri?*" he asked. "It's quite a serious issue in the Courts, but is it so very serious in your profession? I mean, you have the plea of privileged information—though whether this issue's ever been tested as between doctor and corpse I just don't know."

"In the nineteen fifties and earlier, it would have been a quite serious charge to have been laid against a registered practitioner," replied Tina. "Nowadays—the way things are going in matters of sex and morality, I just don't know. One could even get commended for one's liberal-minded and permissive attitude, whereas thirty years ago or less it would have meant the chop. I'll have to wait and see. Anyhow, I'm leaving it all to Jan Barden and her partner Dickie Moore."

Struthers nodded approval. "You couldn't do better, Tina," he said. "They're both first-class people. Ah, here come the second round of martinis."

The dining room of the hotel was on the ground floor, and it opened out onto a terrace that was roofed with grapevines, through which the stars twinkled most accommodatingly; the heavenly galaxy was completed by a full moon, which, with admirable stage management, had been placed a hand'sbreadth above the horizon and in dead centre of the Gulf of Salerno. The night was warm. Out across the still water, the lights of the village shrimp boats crawled slowly like fireflies. Down below, someone was strumming on a guitar.

"It is so perfect," said Tina, "as to be almost a parody."

He agreed.

To begin, they had baby mussels, taken from the rock pools below, marinated in a brew of garlic, lemon, and saffron, and served on thin slivers of toast dipped in garlic. Both offered up brief prayers for survival and collapsed in giggles. For the first time since she had met him at

Heathrow, Tina felt completely at ease with the many-faceted creature who made up Marcus Struthers, Q.C.

With the mussels—champagne . . .

They touched their tall glasses together.

"To—what?" asked Tina.

"To you, of course," he responded. "To us, also. And, as a little coda—to my K."

"Your K?"

"I had a discreet note from the chap in the Prime Minister's office this very morning before I met you," he said, "asking whether I would accept a knighthood if offered in Her Majesty's Birthday Honours List. Not unnaturally, I accepted."

"Well, this is worth the toast," said Tina, "and now we shall all have to get used to addressing you as 'Sir Marcus.' Seriously, I'm very happy for you, Marc. I know the honour's richly deserved. It means a lot to you, doesn't it?"

He nodded and looked down into his glass.

"Yes," he said. "I don't want to pull the hearts-and-flowers pitch, but I wish my old mum were alive to see this day. She didn't actually take in washing to put me through school and university, but she was an ever-present goad to my ambitions. Whenever I flagged, there was Mother to point to the miserable street where we lived and remind me of the patrimony to which I was truly heir—I'm a bastard, you see, Tina —and it was back to his books for little Markie."

She reached across and touched his hand.

"I knew a little of all this, Marc," she said, "but not all. I'm sorry your mother didn't live to see your great success, but all your friends will be happy for you—and they're many."

"I had hoped," said he, "that you and I could be more than friends, Tina."

The night, the champagne coloured her attitudes to a degree where it was easy to shrug off the allusive remark with a smile.

The next course, served with a grave-faced dedication by a dark-eyed lad in a striped singlet, was tortellini: pasta dumplings stuffed with chicken and ham, and covered with a cream and Parmesan sauce. They laughingly agreed not to change wines midstream and stayed with champagne.

"By the Queen's Birthday Honours, I shall be free," he said, "even given the Law's delays, which in these enlightened times are not considerable."

"What shall you do with your freedom, Marc?" she asked, feeling that she was feasting with a panther, and quite liking it.

"What did you do with yours, Tina?" he countered.

"My ex-husband simply moved up to the top floor," she said. "There was never any question of my being able to throw him out into the street: he would have been found days later, stiff and cold. Poor Jock, alas, was conditioned to a much gentler world than yourself, Marc. A life that began with nannies and nursery maids; then, when his father was translated to India as aide-de-camp to the Viceroy, to a host of ayahs, bearers, coachmen, a footman who always stood behind his chair—a boy of seven—throughout every family meal in the Viceregal palace. Your life, happily, has been all ascendancy; Jock's only elevation has been to the top floor of eighteen Lochiel Street."

They speculated upon relative upbringings till the next course of saltimbocca—sautéed veal escalopes finished in a sherry sauce with ham and Gruyère cheese—and switched to a robust Chianti.

"I think I shall take a sabbatical," said Struthers. "Clawing one's puny way up the ladder of the Law has meant that I've been at it fairly constantly since I was first called to the Bar. I suppose it could be said that devotion to career went a long way to destroying my marriage."

Tina thought of Lady Miriam, and a particular occasion when she had been witness to—indeed, recipient of—that forceful aristocrat's venomous, drunken tongue—and made no comment.

"The South Seas, I think," continued her companion. "Fly to Tahiti or someplace, charter a small schooner with a Kanaka crew, and head for the horizon. How does that strike you, Tina?"

"It sounds tremendous fun."

"It could be quite lonely: just me and the Kanakas."

She laughed lightly and took a sip at her very excellent Chianti. "Oh, you'll find lots of company, Marc. All those beautiful island women, not to mention the hordes of rich divorcées—all aching to hook a distinguished titled Englishman with a yacht."

"Don't mock me, Tina," he said, suddenly serious.

She touched his hand again. "Nor shall I," she said.

From that moment, it seemed to her that there was a certain inevitability about it all. She supposed that her acceptance of the invitation to come to Ravello had carried with it a tacit assumption that, given the right "chemistry," the two of them might become lovers; and the technical, moralistic issue of Marc Struthers's unresolved marital state apart, there was no earthly reason why, as mature and discerning adults, they should not.

The dinner over, they took their glasses of grappa and went down to an enchanting water garden below the terrace: a place of rills and runnels, fed by the mountain springs, that chattered and gurgled down lead-lined conduits, to reappear from the mouths of marble dolphins and to issue from the nipples of alabaster naiads in shallow fountain basins shaped like upturned scallop shells. There was a rhumba combo—muted trumpet, guitar and maracas—playing quite quietly down there beside a minuscule circular dance floor. Tina and Struthers embraced and danced languorously to "Guantanamera," just the two of them, with the rather middle-aged trio nodding and smiling approval; slipping into another Latin-American golden oldie without a break.

Presently, he said: "Sleepy?"

"Mmmm," she replied. "Dreamy, is how I would put it. But not tired."

"Shall we call it a day—so far as the world is concerned?"

She did not reply; merely nodded against his shoulder.

Hand in hand, not speaking, they ascended the steps to the hotel.

What then followed remained etched in Tina May's mind quite sharply and unequivocally.

They passed through the foyer. At the same time there emerged from the dining room, at stage left, a middle-aged couple more formally attired than they: black tie and long frock. They were chatting together in the easeful manner that spoke of a marriage lightly borne.

Struthers immediately tensed. His hand slipped out of hers, and, turning sharply, he walked quickly back in the direction from which they had come and was almost immediately out of sight. The passing couple threw Tina a disinterested glance, went on towards the stairs, and were soon gone.

Puzzled, but only slightly disturbed, Tina waited for half a minute before slowly wending her way to her room. She had barely put the key in the lock when Struthers came swiftly down the corridor towards her: his face was strained, his eyes hunted, and there was something rather loose and disturbing about his mouth.

"Good God, Tina!" he grated. "That was a damned close shave!"

She shrugged, spread her hands, uncomprehending.

He pointed back towards the stairs. "That, believe it or not, was the chap who runs the Prime Minister's office! Fortunately, I'm pretty sure he didn't see me—don't you agree?"

Tina stared at him, unbelieving. Was this the handsome, virile male animal to whom she had almost surrendered herself? This the parfit gentil knight come to sweep her off her feet? What she saw in his face was fear: fear for the bauble of fame that might be snatched from under the eager nose of the little illegitimate boy from the back-street slum. And on the instant of realisation, she felt sorry for him.

"No, I'm sure he didn't see us together," she said. "After all, Marc, I've got a pretty well-known face, and it's certain that either he or his wife would have done a double take and given me the 'You *are* you, aren't you?' routine if they'd recognised me."

The worst of his fear abated, he had the grace to feel ashamed.

"Believe me, Tina, he's the kind of fellow who'd put the worst possible construction on our being here together," he said.

"And you still not divorced," she said. "Yes, I can see your point. If you get caught out with me, you can kiss goodbye to your K."

He winced, and dropped his gaze. "You—you must think I'm pretty cheap, Tina," he murmured.

"Not at all, Marc," she replied. "I would say you put a very high price on yourself. Good night, my dear. Thanks for a lovely evening."

She scarcely slept; but had a bath, changed into slacks and a jumper, packed her suitcase and hold-all, and settled herself down in an easy chair to read a book. Somewhere before dawn, she dropped off into a cat-nap and was awakened by the dawn chorus of birds in the garden below the balcony.

There was a clerk on duty by seven o'clock. She phoned down and had him prepare her bill and call a taxi.

When only the most adventurous of the guests were coming down to breakfast (and Struthers and "the chap who runs the Prime Minister's Office" were not among them), she had settled her bill and was being whisked away to Naples airport.

Dry-eyed, uncomplaining, and on the whole rather relieved, she reasoned this way: the candlelit dinner had been a lure to which she had willingly submitted herself, and it was only by a stroke of chance that she had discovered the real truth about Marcus Struthers: no woman in his life could ever be more than a bad second to his ambition.

With the demonstrable realisation came a quite distinct sense of release.

The killer called Norman, gleaning as he did from the press that his slaying of Mrs. Alice Pouter of Harrow had apparently not been connected with the others, determined upon yet another *modus operandi* in the case of his newest target, the susceptible Mrs. Vallence.

Their first meeting had gone off well: the porings over photographs in her well-appointed "lounge" with its revealing silverware and original oil paintings, the Regency furniture and bric-a-brac (he had an eye for all these, having once briefly worked as an auctioneers' porter), told him that the widow Vallence was, in his phrase, "not short of a bob or two." The visit to the crematorium, likewise, had been fruitful: his modest floral tribute laid alongside hers in the Garden of Remembrance; the touching moment when he and she—the major's widow and the humble sergeant of the Loyals—had joined hands, briefly, tearfully—all good stuff.

After his favourite heavy breakfast in the second-floor flat in Penge, which was not a mile distant from the bathroom in Tooting where Miss Clarice Waterhouse had met her end, and about the same distance from Croydon and the second of the bride-in-the-bath-style cases, the killer Norman decided he would make what salesmen generally refer to as the "follow-up." He went out to a phone booth (he never used the one in the hall of his block of flats) and put a call through to Mrs. Vallence. Their mutual manner of address, the implied intimacy, was proof of the success he had achieved after their return to her well-appointed lounge, and the sales pitch he had put to her.

"Teresa."

"Oh, Norman! How nice of you to ring me. You must have guessed that I felt sort of—well—you know . . ."

"It's only to be expected, Teresa. I know exactly how you feel, and the major would have felt just the same, believe me. But it's no use to go on moping like this, Teresa—living a half-life. You've got to take your fate in both hands and become a real person again. You trust me, don't you, Teresa?"

"Oh yes, Norman. After yesterday, I'd go anywhere with you—*anywhere!*"

"Well, there it is, then. When will you be ready to leave?"

"Oh, it was so easy yesterday afternoon, Norman. But there are practical things that get in the way. Like the cat and dog. Tradesmen's bills. The Women's Institute—what are *they* going to think of me? And the vicar? . . ."

"Well, I'm sure you'll be able to sort all that out, Teresa," he said soothingly. "You'll be going along to the bank this morning to pick up the—you know? . . ."

"Oh, I'm not sure about that, Norman. I think I shall have to wait till things are clearer in my mind. Give me—let me think—give me a week to sort things out. All right?"

"Of course, Teresa. I'll ring you again in a week."

"Till then, Norman. Oh, and . . ."

"Yes?"

"Oh, when you told me, yesterday—and in that wonderful, modest way you have—how you and the major together saved that lost patrol in the desert and drove them to safety in your jeep, with bullets flying all round you—I just knew that I could trust myself in the hands of a man who was just like my darling departed husband. I really think you were sent to me, Norman."

"I know I was, Teresa," he said.

He put down the phone, and took from his pocket the cutting from the *Telegraph* where he had ringed the half-dozen short list of prospects. Beside Mrs. Vallence's entry, he now pencilled in: *Gone off the boil a bit. Perhaps feels guilty? Told her I'd ring her next week.*

Picking out another prospect at random, he inserted his coin and dialled the number.

Tina's flight was on schedule. She arrived back at Lochiel Street in the late afternoon, as Maggie Wainwright was putting on the kettle for tea.

"Gosh, Tina, you're soon back!" exclaimed Maggie.

"I never should have gone in the first place, Maggie," responded the other, throwing aside her baggage and flopping down into a comfortable kitchen armchair. "Nor would I have, but for the medical council, the threat of Jock coming home, and the poor damned cat getting himself run over.

"By the way," she added as the thought struck her, "has Jock? . . ."

Maggie pointed upwards. "Yes, he arrived first thing this morning. Dumped a pile of battered luggage up in the attic bedroom and filled the washing machine with a double load of filthy clothes. Then he borrowed ten pounds off me and left."

Tina fumbled in her handbag for her wallet and took out a ten-pound note, which she passed over to her companion. "Take it," she said. "I might as well pay you back now as later—for Jock never will. And for heaven's sake, don't ever lend him a penny-piece again. The sordid business of repaying loans simply doesn't feature in the ethic of my ex."

Maggie wrinkled her nose and looked thoughtful. "He was absolutely charming to me," she said. "And I'm not a girl who falls for a smooth line and a Greek profile—but he really is something, Tina." She ruffled her crisp, short-cut hair, a habit she had when she was thinking. "What's the catch with him?"

"The catch with him is that he's got the talent and intellectual equipment to be a successful writer," replied Tina, "but is of the opinion that his real métier lies in making a fortune by his wits. In the pursuit of which"—she ticked off the items on her fingers—"in the pursuit of which he has: been into a scheme to build an atomic plant in the Arctic to control the weather in the Northern Hemisphere—that got no further than a lot of well-illustrated prospectuses paid for by the proceeds of selling my engagement ring; bought himself into a foolproof scheme to desalinise the Red Sea and turn the Persian Gulf into a land flowing with milk and honey—for that he did eighteen months in an Arab jail. Oh, and he's got a permanent lien upon raising the *Titanic* and building a transatlantic tunnel."

They laughed. Maggie poured tea, and Tina buttered a crumpet.

"What else happened overnight, Maggie?" she asked.

"Nothing," said the other. "I phoned the TV people and told them you'd be out of the country for a few days, but there's no panic there, since you've already got three shows in the can."

"Oh heavens, Maggie! I quite forgot to ask you to cancel my visit to Jamie Farrell's on Friday—not that it matters, because I shall be able to keep the appointment after all."

"Oh, he's the dishy guy with the polly parrot who was on the one o'clock programme last week. Yes, I remember your telling me you had lunch with him. What's he like?"

Tina drained her teacup and poured them both another.

"Firstly, my dear," she said, "he is not by any stretch of the imagination 'dishy.' In normal social congress—like over a lunch table, or having a casual drink—he is a pain in the social neck. But I have to say that, when he has control of a hawk on his glove, he becomes something—quite—really, I don't know, Maggie . . .

"I don't know how to explain it. And this must have been what came across to you when you saw him on the TV spot. Yes?"

"Very strongly, Tina—very strongly indeed. He's—terrific."

The killer Norman, working his usual sales pitch on the next prospect on his short list (the widow of a rich Birmingham industrialist), made the first grade and was invited round for tea. The lady in question, one Mrs. Carruthers, had a most receptive mind and, after some light dalliance, was persuaded that Norman's proposition was a good idea.

After all, what had she to lose? Money can't buy love, nor can cheerless empty years ever become a simulacrum of the heady days when one was young, much desired and—not to mince matters—frequently taken.

Mrs. Carruthers gladly succumbed to Norman's importunities, for she was sick and tired of living alone and unwanted, and his offer presented images of fresh woods and pastures new. Unfortunately, there was a snag which she did not communicate to Norman. The late Mr. Carruthers, industrialist, when he realised that his time was coming, and making a shrewd guess as to how his wife would whistle through his fortune when he was gone, put checks and balances on the disposal of the cash flow and an absolute embargo on the sale of real estate. The arrangement over the cash flow—which caused Mrs. Carruthers a lot of annoyance and personal inconvenience—was that for any withdrawal over a thousand pounds, she had to give her bank manager one week's notice. It always seemed to her an absurd and humiliating—and indeed meaningless—procedure. It was far from meaningless.

The week's moratorium was devised so that the bank manager had time to apprise her stepson, Mr. David Carruthers, about the incursion upon the cash flow—and, if necessary, allow him to impose some restraint upon his stepmother.

The next day—Friday—Mrs. Carruthers went along to her bank and informed the manager that she wished to withdraw no less than five thousand pounds from the current account in a week's time; which enabled her stepson (no friend of hers) to make certain enquiries.

FIVE

Tina did not own or use a car in London, preferring taxis and finding them cheaper and more convenient. For out-of-town jaunts, she usually hired a car from a Chelsea garage just round the corner.

On Friday afternoon, she set off in the loan motor and drove to that part of Essex which is largely comprised of ticky-tacky retirement bungalows, smallholdings and chicken farms, petrol stations, run-down light industrial concerns, and telegraph posts.

And yet, all unexpectedly (and this is a curious feature of the English countryside, which is arcane and inward-looking even when largely raped), Farrell's place, when she had finally run it to earth at the end of a long and twisting lane, was quite charming: a long, low-built, single-storey white-washed cottage under a well-thatched roof. Farrell himself was up a ladder and making good the thatch with a bundle of reed when she drove in. He gave her only a casual glance over his shoulder, nor did he come down till he had finished the job.

"You came—after all," he said, unsmiling.

"Did you think I wouldn't?" she countered.

"Come and see the hawks," he said.

Round the back of the cottage was a lawn that was still parched with the frosts of winter. Set upon it were half-a-dozen circular metal perches, from which a row of hostile, flickering glances greeted their arrival.

"They're quite beautiful," said Tina. "Now, tell me what sort they all are."

Farrell had brought his thick leather gauntlet. Slipping it

on, he by some means induced the right-hand bird to step its taloned claws onto his fist, next unfastening the leash which had secured the creature to the perch and wrapping it between his fingers.

"She's an intermewed goshawk," he said. "Which means she moulted in captivity. See the horizontal striped marking on her breast? That's the adult marking. With the eyas, on the other hand, the breast markings are lighter in colour and heart-shaped—like your friend Baby, here." He pointed to the hawk perched alongside the other, who stiffened when Tina made a move to touch her.

"Hello again, Baby."

"Not bad," said Farrell. "You just might have a natural way with hawks. A lot of eyases would have bated away like mad at anyone making a silly move like that."

Tina did not reply, accepting the mixed compliment with good grace.

There were more introductions: to a peregrine falcon, sleek and black-eyed; two kestrels and a sparrowhawk; a saker. They all had the same watchful attention to the humans and each seemed poised on the end of a screaming nerve.

"We'll go down to the paddock and try the gos on a lure," said Farrell.

The paddock was in a dip at the rear of the cottage, about three acres of rough grassland where a donkey grazed. A stream ran down through the middle and the whole was ringed with rather sick-looking elm trees. It was to an upper branch of one of these that Farrell sent the goshawk, releasing her from the leash which was attached to short strips of leather attached to each ankle. The bird took her place up there, ruffled her feathers, yawned, and settled down to watch events with the air of someone who has seen the show score of times before and quite likes the plot.

The falconer had brought with him a thing of wood and leather with rather battered birds' wings attached to each of its four corners. From a satchel he then produced a hunk of raw meat and tied it to the contraption.

"Watch this," he said. "This is part of a hawk's training, to get 'em to come to the fist. The food's everything, for the damned things don't come to you because they like the colour of your eyes—but because you've trained 'em to regard you as their universal provider. You start with this thing, which is called the lure."

They both took up place in the middle of the paddock, about a hundred yards from the still figure perched up in the leafless elm. Farrell then began to spin the lure at shoulder height on the end of a length of cord, gradually increasing the length till it was describing generous circles about them both.

"Watch the birdie," he said. "This is old stuff to her, and strictly for your benefit. If you bat an eyelid, you'll miss the best bit."

One more circle, and the goshawk plunged from her eyrie and came skimming low over the grass towards where they stood. Tina caught her breath, to see the flashing yellow eyes, the tensed talons, the powerful beat of the wings, the spread tail. Timed to an instant, the computer brain within the narrow skull making the swift mathematical calculation of speed, distance, and relative angles of approach, the hawk struck at and grabbed the circling contraption of wood, leather, and raw meat and bore it to the ground.

When they reached her, she was standing on the lure, her cruel talons buried into the meat, from which she was tearing large chunks with her curved beak; notwithstanding this, when Farrell presented his fist, she flew to it without demur. There was still blood upon the curve of the goshawk's beak.

"And that," said Tina, "would have been a prey?"

"Yes," he said. "Stone cold dead—and eaten."

"It's cruel."

"Life's cruel. Death's less than cruel."

"Notwithstanding," she said, "I think she's beautiful." And she touched the barred breast of the goshawk, who was taking a reward of meat from her master's fist; the predator briefly looked up and accepted the gesture in perfect accord.

"You'd make a good falconer," he said. "There's an elemental ruthlessness about you—no matter how you try to push it to one side."

His Viking face was close; the blue-grey eyes—so like the colour of the North Sea—held no warmth, only challenge. For one moment, she imagined that he would stoop and kiss her upon the lips; but he did not. Nor had she formulated any defence against him.

"I suppose," she said, "that my next lesson will be to watch the kill—the real kill?"

He shrugged. "Let it wait till next time you come." He stroked the goshawk's breast. "She'll kill any time on demand. That's nature."

+++*TOSTIG, Artur. Occupation musician. Born Bradford, Yorks, 1934. Height 5' 10". Declared homosexual. Sentenced Ely Magistrates' Court 10-1-80 for Driving While Under the Influence. No other convictions. Attempted suicide by barbiturates but resuscitated Middlesex Hospital 23-12-81. N.H.Insurance, Car Licence details follow*+++

This preliminary print-out from the Central Criminal Register, which in the United Kingdom embraces almost everyone who has been convicted of anything from a small parking offence upwards, and is of the sort obtainable at any central police headquarters around the country by pressing a button, arrived in West Kensington within minutes of it having been established that the identity of the male person who had fallen from the top floor of an apartment block in the area was the owner of the apartment from which the "defenestration had initiated" (this, in the language of Shakespeare and Milton, is the officialese which is used to describe the act of throwing oneself, or being thrown, from a window to one's death). Only the fact that suicide was suggested in the print-out directed a copy to the desk of Detective Sergeant Turner at New Scotland Yard, who did a little more checking around and then went to see his chief.

"Sir, this could be a connection," he said.

"Spell it out to me," responded Arkwright. "And nothing fancy."

"Different *modus operandi,* I grant you," said the other. "But that's only to be expected. Having, as he might think, got away with two bride-in-the-bath methods, our man's now turning to defenestration."

"By your smug looks," said Arkwright, "I discern that you must have fuller and better proof than the wild assertion which you have just thrown at me in the pious hope that I shall swallow it whole in one mouthful."

Smugly, Turner responded: "Yesterday, Tostig, who, as you must know, sir, is one of the most famous flute-players— what they call a 'flautist'—in the world—drew out from his personal, current account the sum of five thousand pounds cash."

"In his kind of income bracket," said Arkwright, "that could be peanuts."

"Maybe, sir," said Turner, "but Tostig is known to be a tightwad. He once sued a manservant of his for the return of a dinner jacket which, as he alleged, had been loaned as uniform. And he got it back."

"And where is this five thousand—don't tell me—it's nowhere to be found?"

"His flat was gone through with a toothcomb, and a lot of dubious material brought to light—videos, sound tapes, photos and so forth. The local police were following up the homosexual jealousy angle. But not a penny-piece did they find."

Arkwright nodded. "We'll accept the case—tentatively— in the bath-murder syndrome," he said. "And you'd better get Dr. Tina to do the post-mortem."

"Sooner her than me," said Turner, grimacing.

"Why do you say that?"

"The guy fell six floors from his penthouse. And landed across the ornamental railings in the forecourt."

"There was a call this morning from Tony Dacres," said Maggie, "inviting you to a party round at his place on Monday, and will you bring a partner because they're overflowed with women."

Dacres had been a student with Tina and was now a renowned neurologist with a Harley Street consultancy.

"Difficult," said Tina. "I'm a bit low on men at present."

Maggie tapped her cheek and looked ceilingwards. "You could take your bird-man," she suggested.

"Jamie Farrell?" exclaimed Tina. "To a high-flown medical shindig in Harley Street? Why, Maggie, the poor fellow's scarcely house-trained."

"Well, you could take your ex-husband. He's due back any day—or so we're led to believe. His washing's all dry and ironed—by me."

"Tony knows Jock," said Tina. "Need I say more?"

"Also," said Maggie, consulting her notebook, "Detective Chief Inspector Arkwright's office rang. Will you please do the P.M. on Artur Tostig?"

"Oh yes, I saw the piece about him being killed."

"Mr. Arkwright will be present at the P.M. I was asked to tell you that the death has been tentatively docketed along with Detective Sergeant Turner's famous brides-in-the-bath cases. That's how I had the message—they said you'd know what it meant."

"Interesting. Where's the P.M. to be held?"

"Borough District."

"Oh! Pity."

"I was also asked to tell you that the attendant Skerrit's been laid off on full pay. At his own request, and with his union's approval."

"Thank heavens for that. Did they give a time?"

"Any time at your convenience."

"Ring and tell them tomorrow morning at ten, will you,

please, Maggie? But before you do that, I think I'll ring my bird-man—as you call him. I'll ask him to come along to Tony's party."

"I hope I shan't be sorry that I suggested it," declared Maggie.

The taxi was late. For one reason and another Tina felt like death when she reached the mortuary. Arkwright was there, nor did he look in any too good a shape: she discerned his colour to be bad and there was a tell-tale blob of cotton wool on the angle of his jaw that told of a losing encounter with an old-fashioned razor.

"Hello, Tina," he said. "I've got all the lowdown on the Harkness girl business and I want to say I'm as sorry as hell that you've been caught up in a thing like that. I would have rung you before, but I reckoned that you'd rather not talk about it."

"Right, Derek," she said. "Let's forget it. And thanks for the kind thought. What are the indications on this Tostig case?"

"Rich as God," he said. "Highly talented. Genius, so they say. I quote: 'In Gluck's *Orpheus and Eurydice*, Tostig's masterly contribution opens the mind to fresh vistas of immortality'—end of quote. About the rest I can't say, except that it looks like straight suicide. And, of course, Turner's set upon his syndrome. He may be right."

She laid a hand on his arm. "Let's go and see, Derek," she said.

Ohmygawd! . . .

This she said in her mind, never having expressed her view of a cadaver ever since she fainted at her first anatomy lesson. All things pass.

The distinguished flautist, having fallen six storeys on to railings and having been there impaled and removed with some difficulty, and with little skill, presented something of a conundrum to a forensic pathologist. Tina May did the best she was able, conscious all the while that Arkwright at her side was only holding on to his equanimity by sheer will power. She worked quickly and calmly, assisted by old Thursby, who had been with her at the Waterhouse postmortem, and was showing her that special kind of deference which suggested that he disassociated himself from the contemptible Skerrit.

"He was drunk," said Tina. "The stomach's awash with alcohol—can't you smell it, Derek? We'll establish exactly how much from a blood test, but I'd say that he was drunk almost to incapability. And there are the usual signs of alcoholism—underweight—jaundiced—inflammation of the stomach lining—a very bad case."

"He'd had one drunk-driving conviction, Tina."

"I'm not surprised," she replied. "I'm not into the classical music scene, but I think it would repay you to enquire into his recent professional standing from his agent, manager, or whoever. This man was a chronic alcoholic. Do you see the state of the liver? Look. There."

Arkwright nodded numbly.

"Of course, there are successful alcoholic musicians, and always have been," said Tina, still slicing with dexterity. "Just as some of the world's finest painters, actors, men of letters—ha, doctors, even—have been confirmed drunks. But I would have thought that in the area of the performing arts—like playing a flute—a state of advanced drunkenness might be a decided disadvantage. Do you take my point, Derek?"

"Yes, I do, Tina. It does point to a motive for suicide—if his alcoholism had caught up with his career. And he was pretty big, of course. The best. Do you see any signs of struggle, or wounding, before death?"

"No, I don't. Even the throat, you see, which was impaled on the railing, shows no mark of a ligature, or of manual strangulation. The hands are clean, the fingernails also. All I see here is a man who drank himself into a semi-comatose state and then took a header."

"Or was pushed, Tina."

"As you say—or was pushed. And in the state he was in he wouldn't take much pushing."

"You don't think anything else will emerge from the lab tests?"

"Might. But I don't see what else could add up to more than we know already. If it's the issue of murder or suicide you're after, Derek, the evidence is all here for you to see—and it's ambiguous.

"He either fell of his own accord—or someone deliberately shoved him."

Farrell had responded with quite uncharacteristic docility to her phone call inviting him to escort her to the cocktail party, his only concern being what he should wear; she advised a sober lounge suit and tie, and he seemed gratified for her direction.

They met by arrangement in a little pub off Wigmore Street, a stone's throw from Tony Dacres's house. The falconer's bulk was too massive for the suave suiting; she decided she liked him better in his habitual shapeless tweed jacket.

"How are Baby and Company?" she asked.

He grinned. "Fine—they sent their kind regards."

It struck her then: it was the first time she had ever seen him express any sign of pleasure or warmth.

The warmth disappeared when, after having wrestled drinks from the crowded bar and brought them over to their table, he sat down and scowled at her over the rim of his glass.

"So—what's the form tonight, then?" he demanded with a degree of truculence. "And why are you bringing me along?"

"Tony Dacres is an old student buddy of mine," she explained, "and the party's for a group of visiting firemen— more exactly a society of French lady neurologists who're attending a seminar over here. All Tony's chums were asked to bring an extra chap. It's as simple as that."

He looked in no way mollified by her explanation. "Can't see what use I shall be," he complained. "Don't speak French, don't like the frogs, know nothing about neurology . . ."

"But, Jamie, you are—you!" she pointed out. "Quite unique, the one and only Jamie Farrell. I should have reminded you to bring along some pictures of your hawks to show."

He looked wise, dipped into his breast pocket and brought out a substantial leather wallet, tapped it. "Never without 'em," he declared.

She spread her hands. "Well, there you are," she said. "All you have to do is corral a little lady frog neurologist in a corner and show her your pictures. You'll make her trip."

If she had the thought that the concept would amuse him, she was disappointed. The blank wall of stiff defensiveness that he had first put up against her at the TV studio sprang into place, so hard-edged and tangible that she could surely have reached out and probed its unyielding texture.

"Don't make a joke of this," he said. "To you and your sort, I may be the guy who plays around with dickie-birds— but to me this is serious. This"—he tapped his pocket into which he had replaced the wallet—"is the truth behind appearances, the reality beyond the seemingly apparent. It's the key to life—and death!"

And that, thought Tina, is one hell of a way to start an evening!

Dacres was a bachelor, and shared a luxury flat-cum-consulting rooms with a cousin of his who was in the same line. The party, which was on the mezzanine floor of a handsome Georgian house half-way up Harley Street, was quietly under way when they arrived. A tape of gentle Baroque music scarcely broke through the subdued murmur of voices and the gentle tinkle of glassware.

Their host greeted them, kissing Tina. "We're all loving your show, darling," he said. "It must surely run forever."

"This is Jamie Farrell," said Tina by way of introduction.

The two men shook hands. Tony Dacres gave Farrell the quietly speculative glance he deserved, no more; the falconer held on to the other's grasp a little harder and a little longer than convention required. It was almost a challenge.

Dacres, having extricated himself, put an arm round Tina's shoulder. "I must talk to you, darling," he said. "Now. Right away. Most important. Do you mind?"

"Of course," she responded, intrigued.

Their host waved over an intense-looking young man who was lolling alone by the wall nearby, and introduced him to Farrell.

"You guys grab some drinks and we'll be over to see you later," said Dacres. "Come, Tina." And he led her away by the hand, leaving the other two men together. "Crikey, Tina —what a peasant that chap is!" he murmured close by her ear. "Where did you dig *him* up?"

"Oh, Jamie's all right," she replied, having no wish at all to stand up for Farrell's gaucherie. "It's just that he's never got around to being house-trained yet."

"You certainly can pick 'em, dear," said her companion. "And, speaking of which, I have to tell you that Jock's been around town with his begging bowl—in case you didn't know yet."

"Oh no! How much did he touch you for, Tony?"

"He tried for a hundred, but slid out of the game at twenty. He'll give you a bad name around the place, Tina."

"Is that what you wanted to talk to me about—just Jock?"

"No, dear," replied Tony. "It's a mite worse than even your troubles over Jock. It's about your summons before the Medical Council." Taking a couple of glasses of champagne from a passing waiter, he gave one to her.

"Is that all over town, too?" she asked.

"Not quite," he replied. "I heard about it only through my old man, who's a member of the council, as you know. No, it's all been kept fairly well under wraps insofar as they're concerned. Dog doesn't eat dog, not in our noble calling at any rate. At least, that's been the general rule one's come to accept. There won't be any prior leakage to the press, so my daddy says, and only the briefest of statements after the enquiry. At least"—he eyed her over the rim of his champagne glass—"that is the pious hope."

"What are you getting at, Tony?" she demanded.

"As a matter of principle," he said, "the council would never have soiled its fingers with any report that was initiated by a rag like the *Sunday Courier*. You want to kill your wicked stepmother in full view of the commuters milling around Oxford Street Underground on a Friday evening, but don't want the Medical Council to take it up? Make sure it's featured in the *Courier* on Sunday.

"I speak in jest, of course; but there's a core of real truth in it. My old man tells me—and I've no reason to believe that he's lying—that the general feeling on the council was to turn a blind eye to the whole affair, in the hope that it would quietly go away.

"Alas, however, a certain member called an extraordinary meeting, laid the report in front of them—together with the true transcript of Skerrit's affidavit—and demanded that you, Tina, be summoned before the Preliminary Proceedings Committee, to answer the charge of *suppressio veri*."

Tina, who had been listening with growing unease, looked him straight in the eye. "But—who, Tony?" she demanded. "Who'd do such a thing to me?"

"Warburton-Fosse."

"Him?" she breathed. "Of course—who else?"

"No friend of yours, so I take it, Tina?"

"You could say that," she replied.

A near-contemporary of Johnny Kettle, Warburton-Fosse and the grand old man of British forensic pathology should have marched side-by-side as standard bearers and proclaimers of the truth in the bad old days between the wars when the message of their exciting new medical science was so hard-fought in the courts of the land, and it was only the Olympian personality of one practitioner—or two at most—which had won any credibility with the sceptical hanging judges of the old school, who believed only what they saw with their own eyes plain—preferably to five places of decimals.

Kettle and Warburton-Fosse, second generation of the new giants, working in concert, could have carried all before them: secured the acceptance of forensic-pathological principles twenty—thirty—years earlier than had come about—if only they had sung with the same voice. Warburton-Fosse would have none of it.

Jealous of his own *amour propre,* his personal standing in the courts and in the press; jealous, most of all, of Johnny Kettle for his ease of manner, his popularity with men and women alike, his air of profound scholarship lightly borne, the affectionate iconoclasm with which he viewed his noble family—for these and other things Warburton-Fosse had one attitude to Kettle: and that was to best him at every turn.

The courts—and even the press—grew cynically weary of seeing the two giants tearing their own and each other's evidence apart in some of the most sensational criminal cases of the late 1930s, the war years, and the fifties. Nor was Johnny Kettle blameless, for he dearly loved a scrap, and his fundamental distaste for Warburton-Fosse, coupled with the guilty knowledge of what they had wrought between them, had goaded him into participating in the last extravagant phase of mutually destructive court appearances.

It was only in the last ten years of his life that Johnny Kettle found his peace; with Warburton-Fosse discredited at last, his specious theories in rags, there was simply no one left to fight anymore. Johnny relaxed. Wrote. Broadcasted. Found Tina—the wife and daughter he had never had.

No such consolations awaited the old age of Warburton-Fosse. He was left with only the bitter gall of resentment.

"No friend of mine," repeated Tina. "I remember the first time we crossed swords. It was at an exhumation, and I'd been given a watching brief by Janet Barden, representing the husband of the deceased. There was a strong question of foul play. When Warburton-Fosse rumbled who I was and my connections with Johnny, I had the clear notion that, no matter what the truth of the issue—whether someone should go free, or have his life ruined—his primary concern was to get the better of me. Nothing else mattered. Nasty man."

"Well, at any rate," said Tony Dacres, "it was he who brought the matter before the council meeting, and the council could ignore it no longer. Father says the fellow had already formed a cabal to support his motion for you to be summoned to appear before the Preliminary Proceedings Committee. The motion went through on the nod.

"And he's got himself on to the Preliminary Proceedings Committee, for the occasion, Tina."

"I appear to be trussed and ready for the oven," she responded. "And I think I'd like some more champagne, please, Tony."

Whether it was that the group of French lady neurologists had brought with them a particularly pernicious form of feminism, or whether the polarity of cultural and other attitudes which so sadly bedevil relationships between the Anglo-Saxons and their nearest neighbours was more than usually intense that evening, it was soon obvious that Tony Dacres's optimistic mix had failed to jell. The Frenchwomen stuck together at one corner of the room; whenever a British male ventured into the group, he was subtly seized upon by a single member and drawn away to a quiet spot; a few minutes' halting conversation—and he found himself alone again.

Jamie Farrell was never offered the opportunity to show his hawk photos, but remained throughout the party in low-voiced but heated conversation with the intense-looking young man to whom he had been introduced; or, rather, it was Farrell who made most of the running; the other listened to his companion with an expression of ever-increasing incredulity and shook his head quite a lot.

Considerably quenched by Dacres's news about the council, Tina resigned herself to enduring till the time came for a strategic withdrawal that lay within the parameters dictated by an old friendship gone a little tired: eight-fifteen seemed just about right. Meanwhile, in a quite distinguished and largely medical gathering, she wore the cachet of a TV personality and never lacked for the company of the kind of men and women who might otherwise have dismissed her as a run-of-the-mill forensic pathologist who had been invited along on account of her good looks. Fawned upon and flattered by the sort of folks whose attitude to the TV medium is usually one of amused contempt, but who were enchanted to encounter her three-dimensional manifestation, Tina eked out her last half-hour very pleasantly.

When the time came, she collected Farrell, thanked Dacres, and was struggling into her coat (no help from her escort: he had forged on ahead), when she chanced to overhear a most disturbing exchange between her host and the intense-looking young man who had been with Farrell all evening. Their voices came to her quite clearly through a light screen of hanging coats:

"Tony, that chap I've been talking to . . ."

"Mmmm?"

"Know anything about him?"

"No. He came with Tina May. Why do you ask?"

"He's got some damned odd views—the sort that could get him into trouble if he aired them abroad."

"We all have our little foibles, Dickie. Maybe he's got the good sense only to air them before the sympathetic ear of a doctor. Anyhow—what's his problem?"

"His problem is that, by any criterion you'd choose to apply, he's stark, staring mad—and should be locked up!"

SIX

The desk sergeant at the Meresham Road Police Station looked up when the woman came in through the swing doors and made his instant appraisal: mid-fifties, good tweed suit, reptile-skin shoes and handbag to match, blue rinse, careful make-up not overdone, and a hat. The hat clinched it: she was upper-crust Finchley, with a retired stockbroker, company director, or career officer for a husband.

She looked around her rather nervously; he had the notion that, having screwed up her courage to come in, it would not take much to get her running right out. Not used to the inside of a nick—save through the medium of TV.

"Can I help you, ma'am?"

His query seemed to settle her resolve. She smiled at him quite coolly and with assurance.

"I have a small, personal problem, sarn't," she said.

(Her manner of contracting "sergeant" clinched it: hubby was a retired officer.)

"Indeed, ma'am—and how can we be of help?"

She hesitated. "I wonder if—would it be possible to speak to a woman officer?"

"Of course, ma'am. If you'll take a seat, I'll arrange for the duty WPC to interview you privately. And your name, ma'am?"

"Vallence—Mrs. Teresa Vallence."

"Won't keep you waiting more than a few minutes, Mrs. Vallence."

Woman Police Constable Daisy Burton shook hands with Mrs. Vallence, ushered her into the Interview Room 2, and made her own summation of the newcomer as she took her seat across the plain deal table: fifty-sevenish, model suit, Gucci shoes and bag, Paris gloves. Over-made-up to the point of looking tarty, and displaying a girlie-girlie cuteness that must be the delight of the prowling old gentlemen in the golf club bar on Sunday mornings.

"Mrs. Vallence, how can I help you?" asked Daisy Burton briskly.

The other dropped her gaze most becomingly and let her false eyelashes flutter for a couple of breaths before she replied. "I'm afraid," she said at length, "that I may have inadvertently done something rather silly."

"Well, we all make mistakes," responded the other. And had the thought that the woman might have come to own up to last Saturday night's hit-and-run on the North Circular.

"It began," said Mrs. Vallence, "with the announcement I put in the *Telegraph* on the anniversary of the major's—my husband's—death."

She went on to tell briefly how the announcement had attracted a telephone call from one Sergeant Wake, formerly of her late husband's regiment; how they had together laid their tributes in the Garden of Remembrance, and returned again to Parkway Close for sherry and *petits fours* . . .

It was at this stage that Mrs. Vallence appeared to suffer a mental block, or check, to her account. She looked to the WPC as if for a lead; Daisy Burton did not oblige her, but instead went off at a tangent: "Mrs. Vallence, can you describe this man—this perfect stranger who rang you up out of the blue, claiming to have served with your husband?"

Mrs. Vallence seemed grateful for the diversion. "Well," she said, "he looked the part to a T. The NCO type, of course, and not a gentleman. But extremely civil and correct in his manners—as might be expected from a man who had served in a good regiment and had absorbed the examples of his leaders. As to looks—I would say strongly, even craggily, built. Not handsome as the world judges handsome men"— her face took on a wistful appearance—"but with the looks of a man who has fought hard, and played hard. There was about him a quite definable air of—*masculinity.*" She almost whispered the word, and let it die away in silence somewhere above the table top between them. "Do you mind if I smoke?" she added.

"Go right ahead," replied WPC Burton.

Mrs. Vallence produced an elaborate gold cigarette case and lighter combined. Daisy Burton having declined an offer, she lit herself one and drew in the smoke luxuriantly. The police officer observed that the first two fingers of the other's right hand were heavily nicotined, and that the taloned red fingernails were of the false, stick-on sort.

To bring matters to a point, the interviewer decided upon another tactic: "Mrs. Vallence, if you are satisfied that your visitor was who he claimed to be, for what reason have you come here to seek our help?" she asked.

Mrs. Vallence looked shifty, and examined the end of her cigarette. "The question of—money—arose," she replied.

"I see. He demanded money from you. With menaces? Blackmail, perhaps?"

The other looked affronted. "What possible cause could he have to blackmail *me?*" she shrilled. When the other did not reply, but continued to gaze evenly at her, the fury abated. "The question arose of our going away together," she continued in a mild tone.

"Wasn't that rather sudden?"

"I—I suppose so."

"Where were you going, Mrs. Vallence?"

"Spain was suggested."

"Whose suggestion was this?"

"His—Norman's."

"He sounds—very persuasive."

"He was—very persuasive." The older woman dropped her gaze, and there was no false coquetry in the gesture. "I don't know what came over me. I let myself be—very silly with him," she whispered.

It added up to this—or so WPC Daisy Burton reckoned it: the persuasive Norman had indulged in a little light seduction that had stopped well short of the bedroom door, but which had held out to this lonely widow—this faded beauty on the verge of a solitary old age—the high promise of passion that would illumine her eventide. Goodbye to Finchley and the roundelay of the golf club, the parish church, the Women's Institute, the cat and the dog, whist drives on the first Friday of the month. Replace that with nights in the gardens of Spain, manzanilla to the clack-clack of castinets— and in company with a rough man with the looks that told of a hard-fought, hard-played life.

It was a vision that had admitted doubts while still the ecstasy remained: Norman had been perhaps a little too insistent upon her immediately drawing out a fairly large sum of money (five thousand pounds) to start the enterprise. By the time he had phoned her the following day, prudence had already intervened amidst the passion, and she had asked for a week to "get things clearer in her mind."

Another couple of days, and she was willing to admit to herself that she might—just might—have fallen into the hands of an adventurer.

There was nothing the police could do at this stage, nor was Daisy sufficiently convinced to take the matter higher up. Norman's promise to phone at the end of the week suggested a tactic to the young WPC.

"When he calls, Mrs. Vallence," she said. "Make a date to meet him in a public place—say the cocktail bar at the Finchley Arms.

"Then ring me. And we'll take it from there."

Tina's reaction to the comment she had overheard about Jamie Farrell's mental state was that the speaker had gone over the top about the falconer's admittedly vehement and aggressive views on the issue of life and death—as he had himself expressed them to her on every occasion they had met, and as recently as that same evening. She could well imagine Jamie, fired with a few champagne cocktails, leading off about nature red in tooth and claw—and maybe declaring that the harsh, pure ethic of the animal kingdom was infinitely to be preferred to man's effete vileness to his fellow man.

Yes, that sounded just like Jamie Farrell at his dottiest. What a man. What an upstream swimmer!

This had occupied her mind during the taxi ride back to Lochiel Street that night. Jamie, who had brusquely refused her offer of supper back at the house, had declared his intention of walking to catch his train back to Essex ("Can't wait to get this foul air out of my lungs").

Maggie was in the kitchen, eating a chicken salad, a copy of a glossy fashion magazine propped up in front of her. She looked round, wide-eyed, when Tina came in.

"Jock's back again!" Pointing up at the ceiling.

"Sober?"

"I wouldn't know. I don't know what he's like drunk."

"You don't need any previous experience. If his condition didn't immediately and forcibly strike you—then he's sober. Thank God!"

"He said he's flying to Scotland tomorrow morning."

"Tomorrow morning—when?"

"Early, Tina. He said early."

Tina went to the fridge, brought out a portion of homemade cottage pie, and put it in the oven. She then poured herself a glass of sparkling Burgundy.

"I don't have to go out till ten o'clock," she declared, "so I shall lie low till he's gone. And I would earnestly advise you to do the same."

Alas for her hopes of avoiding any kind of encounter with her ex-husband! She was woken by a hammering on her bedroom door, and this from a sleep so profound that, having fought her way up through many layers of oblivion, she was calling out aloud in alarm—and the pounding still continuing—before she took stock of herself and remembered her resolve to lie doggo.

"What's the matter—what is it?" She had already betrayed herself.

"It's me—Jock."

"Oh, hello, Jock. I heard you were back."

"May I come in?"

"No."

In the silence that followed, she guessed that he was pulling one or other of the faces that he had perfected for such occasions of rebuff: either the wolf-man face or the Christian-to-the-lions face.

Presently: "I'm off to Scotland—and I might not be back."

"Have a good journey."

"Aren't you going to ask me what I'm planning to do up there?"

"What are you planning to do up there?"

"Well—it's like this. I don't know if you remember Dickie Heffer, who used to captain the Old Boys Eleven. Dickie's old man owned a chain of theatres in the north-east, so naturally the lad gravitated towards show business . . ."

The tune—the same. Only the lyric slightly different, the names changed. Tina closed her eyes and let his sales pitch well over her like warm molasses. The plot unfolded. This time it was supplying live concert parties to the North Sea offshore oil rigs. And why live? Good question. Because the guys out there were sick of the sight of each other, and bored to suffocation with their electronic toys—their space-war games and their ghetto-blasters, porno-video and discos, the television most of all. What their essentially simple spirits craved for was live entertainment—and that was just what Dickie and he were going to bring them. The real stuff: stand-up comics and really good singers and instrumentalists. But—most of all—GIRLS, GIRLS, GIRLS! This had been the formula for the northern workingmen's clubs which had set a pattern for a whole new proletarian culture.

"So what do you think, Tina? Still plenty of room left on

the ground floor if you're interested. Like to chip in a few grand and watch your investment grow overnight?"

"My accountant wouldn't let me," lied Tina. "He's got every penny sewn up and he just gives me pocket money."

"Too bad, Tina. You're really going to be sorry, I promise you."

"What time's your plane, Jock?"

"Yes—yes! I must dash. Well—'bye again, Tina. I expect we'll meet again one day."

"Yes, I expect so," she answered with a certain dull resignation at the pre-ordained and inevitable. "Till then, Jock."

He was gone. She heard him clout down the stairs and along the passage, bumping into everything he passed—walls, bannisters, door frames—with his suitcase and his massive bulk. Jock was incapable of getting into a car without denting the bodywork.

Tina was under contract to perform an unspecified number of post-mortems annually on behalf of the Coroners' Court of South-West London. In fact the arrangement—though ill paid—was a sinecure because these contracts had been handed out to half-a-dozen other forensic pathologists in private practice, the idea being to create a pool of first-class people so that there would always be someone available at short notice.

Mr. Linstock ruled at the South-West Mortuary. Mr. Linstock was the Chief Supervisor: white-coated and impeccable, with a clean, starched collar daily and a discreet spray of flower and fern from his Camberwell garden worn in a metallic slide in his buttonhole; side hair carefully darkened and brushed across his bald pate, waxed moustaches like antennae.

" 'Morning, Mr. Linstock."

"Good morning, Dr. May." The chief supervisor rose from behind his old-fashioned roll-top desk and gave a brief bow from the waist. "I 'ope as 'ow I see you well, ma'am."

"Very well, thank you, Mr. Linstock. And yourself?"

"Mustn't grumble, ma'am. Mustn't grumble."

"Well, what have you got for me this morning?"

The other consulted a clipboard, upon which was penned a list.

"Two subjects—the first an 'eadless corpse taken from the river at twenty hundred hours yesterday. Police suspect gang murder. Ma'am, this subject is already prepared and ready for your examination. Mr. Norman Pierce will hassist."

She supposed that it was a form of self-indulgence to accept a large part of the blame for what had happened to Jock. They had both been so young, though she was light years ahead of him in maturity—even in those days. She should have seen that her very maturity had acted as a spur to the very worst in him, and led him to what he'd become . . .

"Large retractor, Mr. Pierce." The assistant obliged, and lent a hand to the opening of the chest cavity which was still in rigor mortis and stubbornly intractable.

She began to compose in her mind the main outlines of her coming report: it served to shut out Jock Hardacre, that guilty image . . .

Subject, white male. Well nourished, mid-thirties. Height estimated around six feet. Weight around a hundred and eighty pounds. Naked torso missing head and hands. Arms and lower limbs pinioned with ordinary electric flex. Time of death . . .

Jock would not be shut out. The encounter through the bedroom door had been traumatic. She supposed that, in her state of half awakening, she had been particularly susceptible to suggestion, as in the case of a hypnosis subject. And she was suggesting to herself that she should have seen quite clearly that their marriage had set Jock on the downward slope.

"I'll take the full range of specimens, Mr. Pierce, but I don't think they'll show anything."

He had considerable talent as a writer, albeit of the third rate. Left to himself he might have drifted into jolly pot-boilers, made a damned good living and fulfilled all his dreams of the easy life and the company of complaisant women. Instead of which, she—Tina—had acted as a constant goad to the devil within him that said he must compete with her and prove himself, not as a third-rate hack writer, but as a dazzling entrepreneur. A juggler with empires, master of the market-place, a name on every lip.

Heart and lungs sound. No asphyxia. Dead before entering the water (as, headless, he would have to be, wouldn't he?—silly girl!) *No wounds on torso or limbs. No overt signs of poisoning . . .*

Put it this way—the best thing that could have happened to Jock would have been never to have set eyes on me. Best, that he had married some adoring little pudding of thing who would have filled his life with laughter and bouncing babies—and for whom he would have churned out pot-boilers galore, to her never-ceasing wonderment and acclaim.

The presumption is that head and hands were removed to prevent identity. Absence of wounds suggest that subject may have been shot in the head—and presence of slight powder burns on the left shoulder and stump of neck seem to confirm this.

"Fancy a cup of coffee before we go on to the next subject, Doctor?" asked Mr. Pierce.

Tina changed out of her gown, scrubbed up, and joined her assistant in the well-appointed waiting room where there was a tea-and-coffee-vending machine. A uniformed policewoman was there: Mr. Pierce introduced her as Sergeant Hattery. She was fortyish, stout, matronly.

"I'm attending the result of the P.M. on the Green baby, Doctor," she said. Her eyes were a very pale blue and—despite her amiability—watchful.

"The suspect battered baby," said Tina. "My next subject. Can you give me any background, Sergeant?"

"Parents very young. He's nineteen and works on the motorways, earning good money. She's a year younger, what some would call a little slut—and they'd be the charitable ones. Slumps around all day with her hair in curlers, in a dressing gown. Sink full of dirty dishes. Dirty nappies everywhere. Always with a ciggie stuck in her mouth. Dressed and painted up to the nines, though, when she and the hubby go out to a night-club about three times a week. And the neighbours have been talking."

"She sounds like a gift to any talkative neighbour, poor little thing," said Tina. "Did she mistreat the child?"

"Screamed at it," said Sergeant Hattery. "All the day long, the neighbours could hear her howling obscenities at the toddler—how she wished she'd never set eyes on it, how she could smash its head in 'cos it was driving her mad. They could hear her right down at the end of the street—and it's a long street."

"Were any complaints made to the social services people or the NSPCC?"

The WPS looked pityingly at Tina. "The sort of folks who live in Arcadia Street and thereabouts," she said, "they may talk amongst themselves, but they don't go outside. If you ask them why, Doctor, they tell you that they don't want to get caught up in any trouble. That was before the baby was killed. Now—when it's too late—they're vying with each other to sing like birds. And when we question them at the doorstep, they look around in the hope that a TV camera's taking it all in."

"How did the baby die—according to the parents?"

"Fell down the stairs. The mother says the toddler gave her the slip after she'd lifted him out of his bath, and when she looked round, he'd gone. Next thing, she heard a scream, a series of bumps. And the child's lying at the bottom of the stairs with a broken neck."

Tina drained her coffee cup and threw it in the disposal pouch.

"Well, we'll see," she said. "Odd thing about what we now call the battered-baby syndrome, you know, Sergeant. At first it was thought that the alarming increase of fractures in infants was due to a new form of bone disease—but it wasn't. A whole ten years went by with this hypothesis in general acceptance—till a couple of American doctors came up with the outrageous theory that it was the parents or guardians who were doing it all. And they were right."

"Will it take long, Doctor?"

"Not long, Sergeant. The last of these cases I examined revealed multifractures of the skull, a ruptured spleen, evidence of six previous fractures of the ribs, and bruises galore. They weren't difficult to spot. Coming, Mr. Pierce?"

Miss Tewson examined her features in the mirror, and deplored what she saw. A mere fifty-eight years sat uncomfortably upon her countenance and she could pass for a woman ten years older. The ravages of illnesses which had bedeviled her since Father's death—shingles, arthritis and the rest—had reduced her from the active person she had been—prison visitor, active political worker, chairperson of committees galore, regular and loquacious attender at most of the annual general meetings of companies in which she held shares—to the semblance of an invalid, which she indeed was in all but name, being unable to move more than a few steps without a walking frame. The entrapment had been both swift and insidious: one day she was obliged to take to her bed; she emerged from it a month later and had never been outside the front door of her elegant York Terrace apartment since. Moreover, she found herself entirely alone and cut off; the many acquaintances she had made on committee, the party workers, members of her clubs—none of them ever visited her, telephoned her, or sent so much as a postcard. In fact, poor Miss Tewson found herself suffering from the effects of a lifetime of sustained unpopularity. All unknown to herself, what she had always considered to be her great qualities of leadership, her devastating manner of debate, the cool irony with which she had trounced opponents and brought flagging supporters to heel—all these had made her arguably one of the most cordially disliked women in London Society. And now all her swallows had come home to roost.

But today was going to be quite different. And this was why Miss Tewson regarded herself in her mirror as she put on her hat, trying it this way and that: a little to one side, tipped slightly forward over the brow, marginally inclined towards the back of the head and leaving the brow clear and her fringe showing. The hat was of Russian sable, gleaming black as jet, matching her full-length motoring coat. In this ensemble, in the early nineteen sixties, she had driven down to Monte Carlo to stay at the Hotel de Paris, to await the arrival of Father and his team-mate of the Monte Carlo Rally. She could see them now, coming down the Corniche, with the driving snow swirling about their green Aston Martin . . .

As she brushed away a tear that prickled her eye, the front doorbell rang.

"Coming—coming!"

In her clumsy haste, she upset her walking frame and was obliged to sprawl down upon her knees to retrieve it; the clamber up was protracted and painful. Then she was out of her bedroom and framing down the passageway to the door, down the long Isfahan rug that Father had brought back from his last tour of the oil wells.

Don't let him think I'm out, and go away . . .

The bell rang again.

"Coming—I'm coming!"

Panting, Miss Tewson reached the door and drew aside the bolts, detached the chains, unlocked the locks that had kept out the world and her from the world for seven lonely years lightened only by the woman who brought her few provisions and "did" for her, letting herself in by the back door with her own key. *One can't get proper servants today.*

She opened the door. The man who stood on the step was shortish and thickset, smartly dressed in a black suit, white shirt and black tie, black gloves. He wore a peaked cap with a stylised rosette by way of a badge. He smiled and saluted her smartly.

"Miss Tewson, is it, ma'am?"

"You're from the agency in response to my advertisement for a part-time chauffeur?"

"That's right, ma'am. Was you wanting to go for a spin this morning, like?"

"Oh yes—yes! Look—here's the key of the mews garage. The Daimler's in there. You shouldn't have any trouble in starting—I have a man come round from the corner garage who starts her every week and twice a week in winter."

"Right you are, ma'am." He took the key. "I'll have her round here in a jiffy." He turned to go.

"By the way," said Miss Tewson, in the loud and over-emphasised accents that she unconsciously deployed against the lower classes. "What's your name."

"Norman, ma'am," he replied. "Norman—at your service."

The sweep second hand of the clock in the waiting room brought the time to exactly a quarter to one when Tina put her head in the door. She was still wearing a cap and theatre gown. She looked gravely across at WPS Hattery.

"You can turn off the heat and reassure them all in Arcadia Street, Sergeant," she said. "There was no baby battering going on in the Green household."

"But all that shouting and yelling?"

"The poor girl was just letting off steam. She probably wasn't up to the job of mothering, but she made a pretty good attempt for all that. The child was well nourished and perfect in every way—except for a broken neck and bruising consistent with having fallen downstairs."

The motherly WPS looked relieved—but she still had reservations:

"The child could have been pushed . . ."

Tina said, "I'd appear as an expert witness to testify that, given the extensive statistics on the battered-baby syndrome, the probability of a child being murdered by its mother without bearing the slightest traces of previous injury—however small—is virtually negative."

Sergeant Hattery grinned. "Well, that seems to wrap it up, Doctor," she said. "Thanks."

The chief supervisor came in.

"Detective Chief Inspector Arkwright called, ma'am," he said, "and would Dr. May please telephone 'im at the Yard as soon as she's free."

"Thank you, Mr. Linstock."

Pausing only to scrub her hands, Tina phoned Arkwright.

"Tina—how are you fixed for lunch?"

"I thought I'd grab a sandwich and a glass of wine at some pub or other."

"I can offer you a better option than that. Stay where you are and I'll be down in your manor in a quarter of an hour. And, Tina . . ."

"Yes, Derek?"

"Over lunch I'll give you the latest on what is now widely referred to at the Yard as 'Detective Sergeant Turner's Syndrome.' "

"I can't wait to hear," said Tina.

SEVEN

Arkwright was with her inside the quarter hour: slicing through the lunch-hour London traffic in a large police patrol car with its blue light flashing on the roof. He greeted her with a peck on the cheek and handed her into the car.

"Busy morning?" he asked.

"Routine."

He nodded sympathetically. "Ah, this routine!"

"And you, Derek?"

"There's an economy drive on at the Yard. They've brought in a bright boy from outside to trim us down. Quite senior officers are being obliged to make inventories of paper clips in their charge. I'm kidding, of course, but it's nearly as bad as that."

"Where are you taking me for lunch? And, by the way, it really is very kind and thoughtful of you, Derek."

"Tina, for all the work you put in on our behalf, the Metropolitan police should vote you a medal and a slap-up lunch weekly. As for today, I thought you'd be amused by a restaurant close by Cheyne Walk kept by a nut-case who is also a genius in his own line."

"Sounds most intriguing," she said. "Now—tell me about the latest state of Turner's syndrome."

His reply was interrupted by a crackle of static from the front compartment, and a message was relayed and acknowledged by the driver's mate.

"Turner's syndrome is still very much alive," said Arkwright. "Indeed, we've made an official evaluation and put it all on computer. Computer agrees that it hangs together."

"Turner must be pleased."

"Turner's over the moon. He figures that he's now got a straight run home to Police Commissioner. He was very disappointed about Artur Tostig, though."

"Tostig dropped through the syndrome?"

"Straight suicide, undoubtedly," said Arkwright. "I have your tip to thank for giving us the quick answer, Tina. We checked with his agent, one Rosa Savory, a very high-powered lady in the performing world. It seems Tostig's been progressively more of a handicap than an acquisition for quite a while. Last week, he went over the top by turning up drunk for a concert in Budapest. When the dubious quality of his playing won him slow hand-claps, he threw his flute at the conductor and started reviling the regime in no uncertain terms, but was with difficulty hustled over the frontier before the Hungarian political police got wind of the happening. As a result of all that, Rosa Savory dropped him, and all his concert bookings were cancelled. Career finished. Two days later, he took a header from his balcony.

"Ah, we're here, Tina."

"You're dead on time, and not a minute to spare!"

He who addressed them was a short, stout young man with glossy black hair slicked down flat, black boot-button eyes, plump, pasty face, and an angry expression. He was in shirt-sleeves and wore a striped butcher's apron from chest to ankles.

"I booked for one-fifteen, and one-fifteen it is," said Arkwright.

Though there was only the slightest hint of asperity in his tone of voice, it drew forth a reaction from the other that might have been simulated—but did not look it.

"Don't bully me!" he shrilled, eyes staring. "I'll have no police brutality here!"

Arkwright grinned at Tina. "This is our host—Oscar," he said. "He goes on like this all the time and his customers love it."

"How do you do," said Oscar, raising a cool eyebrow at

Tina. "I'm surprised your mother lets you go out with policemen. My mother never permitted it. What are you going to have for starters? You'd better make it something quick and easy. The turbot in port sauce will be ready in five minutes. If you're not ready for *it*, I shall throw it on the floor and you can make do with bread and cheese for all I care."

"I'll toy with a tomato juice," said Arkwright.

"I'll have the same," said Tina.

"Please yourselves," said Oscar, and he flounced off.

"About the wine . . ." Arkwright called after him.

"The wine for turbot is Montrachet seventy-nine," came the reply. "Take it or leave it. You'll defile *my* turbot with nothing else."

"Beneath it all, he really is a marvellous chef," said Arkwright. "Turbot in port sauce is the specialty of the house. I ordered it in the hope you'd like it."

The turbot was a poem. Oscar accepted their compliments as being his due and offered them a forced choice of a gooseberry cheesecake which was as bitter-sweet and uncompromising as the decor of the establishment, which comprised one large, handsome room whitewashed from floor to ceiling, with an elaborate plaster cornice; bare tiled floor, a single aspidistra in an earthenware amphora, and a Victorian steel engraving of Watteau's *Le Débarquement pour l'Isle de Cythère* hung above a marble Adam fireplace. Six tables—and they were the last of the luncheon guests.

"Back to Turner's syndrome," said Arkwright. The consuming of the turbot in port sauce had permitted only sporadic small-talk.

"Tostig is out," said Tina.

"But Waterhouse and Foy are very much in. We bracket them together on three counts. First, the similarity of that old favourite the *modus operandi*. Secondly, the fact that they both drew out large sums of money immediately prior to their deaths."

"So did Tostig," interposed Tina.

"I'll come back to that point later."

"Sorry—please continue." She watched him as he ticked off the points on his fingers: donnish-looking in heavy black library glasses, the eyes registering a keen intelligence, the manner an earnestness lightly borne.

"Neither of the first two points, taken either singly or together, would, in our estimation, connect the two cases— or even suggest that a crime had been committed," he said. "Point three is the evidence that another party was present at both of the deaths.

"There was the heavily built man seen leaving Mrs. Waterhouse's place at the material time, and the undoubted fact that someone thrust Foy's head under water with some force, and then mopped up the floor with a bath towel.

"The clincher is that in both murders—they are now officially murders—there were demonstrable attempts at simulating suicide. In the Waterhouse case, the killer employed Smith's classic method which, for some reason, didn't work with Foy. And I repeat, Tina, that computer agrees with all this." He grinned. "Any questions?"

"I still wonder what happened to the five thousand that Tostig drew out just before his death," said Tina.

"We've figured that he gave it to one or other—or all—of his current boyfriends," said Arkwright. "But he was totally promiscuous, and it would be almost impossible to establish. Computer agrees, and absolutely rejects the money angle as being a significant single point of comparison in so small a sample."

"You mean—if two or three more cases came up, all involving the money angle, they might bring Tostig back into the syndrome?"

"Something like that, Tina."

She shivered. "I think someone just walked over my grave," she said.

Sipping Turkish coffee—scalding hot in tiny cups, sweet as honey, and black as the night—their conversation drifted away from the issues of the Turner syndrome to the matter of Tina's trouble with the Medical Council. She had the thought—perhaps it was the way in which he introduced the topic—that this was the real reason he had invited her out to luncheon.

"The boys back at the Yard are all sorry you're in bad with your medical high-ups, Tina," he said. "They asked me to find out if there was some way we could help." Avoiding her eye, he gazed up at the ceiling.

"That's very kind of you all," said Tina, much affected. "But, since there's no criminal involvement, I'm afraid you could scarcely be of any help. They're hardly likely to suspend me or erase my name from the Register for a single act of omission. The worst that can happen, surely, is that I shall be admonished—and you can bet your sweet life that the *Sunday Courier* will make a meal of it, not to mention David Harkness's political opponents."

Arkwright let a little time go by before he replied:

"This fellow Warburton-Fosse, who put the complaint before the council . . ."

"Oh, you know about that, do you?" exclaimed Tina, surprised.

He looked smug. "Tina, there's not a lot that happens in our manor—particularly to people for whom we've any regard—that slips unseen past the Yard. Yes, we know about Warburton-Fosse's involvement—and quite a lot about the gentleman himself . . ."

Tina fixed his gaze. "Derek Arkwright," she said, "I charge you upon our friendship to stop beating about the bush and say what's on your subtle policeman's mind."

"Tina," he replied, "what I'm going to tell you is a hot potato. You can use it at your discretion, but I'd ask you not to reveal your source. Okay?"

She nodded, puzzled.

"Last September," said Arkwright, "friend Warburton-Fosse was arrested upon a complaint laid against him for kerb-crawling in the West End. It was an open-and-shut case.

The plaintiff was a respectable married woman with family. There were witnesses. The local nick had had previous complaints backed up with the same car number. Are you following me, Tina?"

"Yes, Derek."

"Then it all fell apart. The woman cried off—her husband didn't want any trouble and made her withdraw her statement. The Director of Public Prosecutions dithered around for a while, then decided to drop the case. End of story."

Tina laid a hand on her companion's arm. "Derek, you're not suggesting I should use what you've told me to frighten Warburton-Fosse away?" she asked. "Oh, I think you are! But, my dear, that would be blackmail."

He shook his head. "It would be a hell of a lot less than that, Tina. Put it to your legal advisers. See if they don't think that a quiet word on the side—strictly in private— might give that rat second thoughts about persecuting you."

She shook her head. "I'm grateful for your concern, Derek, and I know you have my best interests at heart. What you've told me confirms me in my belief that Warburton-Fosse is a thoroughly nasty little old man. But I'd be descending to his level—as well as putting your career at risk— if I attempted to lean on him in that kind of way. You do see my point, don't you?" she added, when to her surprise she saw that he was laughing quietly.

"Tina, Tina," he said, "to anyone who knows you, you're so predictable. I told the lads at the Yard, when they pressed me to put this idea to you: 'You don't know Dr. Tina the way I do,' I told 'em. And I was right. You're straight as a die and you walk through this rotten world clean—and there's no filth that can touch you."

"You go on like that much longer, Derek Arkwright," she said, "and you're going to make me cry, damn you."

Maggie was working in her office when Tina got back; she relaxed in her seat and let the word processor do a few little things on its own when her employer came in.

"One Jessica Rothstein rang not ten minutes ago, Tina," she said.

"Did she now?" Tina raised an eyebrow to her reflexion in the wall mirror. *Jeremy's hopefully intended—what's going on?* "What did she want?"

"Sounded a very nice person. Asked can she come and see you some time soon? It's personal—and quite urgent. So—I took a chance and fixed for her to come at six this evening. If you want to chuck, I can ring her right back."

"No, no, Maggie—I'll see her. This is the girl—woman—I told you about. Jeremy's aspiration."

Round-eyed, Maggie regarded her. "Not *the* Jessica Rothstein—little Miss Money-bags? What does she want to see *you* for? Did Jeremy give your name as a reference? Is she seeking a testimonial?"

They enjoyed a good giggle over that.

By six o'clock, when the doorbell rang, Tina had taped her reports on the morning's post-mortems and passed the cassette over to Maggie for transcribing.

Some atavistic impulse had induced her to change out of her sensible, workaday two-piece into a casual but definitively feminine jump suit worn with high heels and some dangly jewellery; she also shook out her ash-blond hair from its habitual trim shape—and supposed the ritual was profoundly significant of something or other.

"Hello—I'm Jessica Rothstein."

"I'm Tina May—do come in."

"What a lovely old house."

"Yes, I'm terribly fond of it. This way. We're in a bit of a mess, I'm afraid. We're doing a spot of do-it-yourself spring cleaning because contractors simply can't be relied upon to turn up when they say they will. Don't touch the handrail, it's wet paint. Oh, I'm so sorry—your lovely gloves!"

"That's all right."

"A dab of thinners will get it off."

"Sure."

"This is my study."

"It's nice."

"Do sit down. I'll fetch the thinners."

Cleaning the white gloss paint from Miss Rothstein's glove was the best ice-breaker around. By the time Tina had poured them both a schooner of Amontillado they had uninhibited eye contact and the vibes were all good.

Tina regarded her visitor over the rim of her glass and saw a handsome woman in her prime. Dark as Tina was fair, with raven hair drawn back into a severe but not unbecoming chignon; luminous dark eyes, a magnolia complexion, exceedingly sensitive and mobile lips, an elegantly sculptured aquiline nose. From what one could see of her figure, it was quite exceptional. When she took off her left-hand glove and placed it with its companion on the arm rest, Tina saw five diamonds winking on the third finger—and recognised the ring at once; it prompted her to step right in and seize the nettle boldly.

"I'm afraid I'm rather remiss in not having written to congratulate you both on your engagement," she said. "Belatedly, I wish you every possible happiness."

"Thank you, Tina," said the other. "I may call you Tina, mayn't I? After all I've heard about you from Jeremy, I feel as if I've known you as long as he has. However," she went on, looking down at her ring, "congratulations though welcome, aren't yet quite in order."

"Oh, why not—er—Jessica?"

"My father doesn't approve. In the grand old Victorian manner, he has withheld his consent—I think that was the phrase our great-grandparents used. In similar vein, he has also cut me off with the proverbial penny."

"Oh no—how awful! Did he give a reason?" asked Tina, and immediately felt a blush of shame and embarrassment begin somewhere in her neck and spread across her cheeks. As she was not much given to blushing, it was a most unpleasant—and hideously revealing—experience.

"Oh, come now, Tina. You can do better than that," said

Jessica Rothstein. "And I thought we were getting on so well and could be frank with each other. It must be very clear in your mind why my father disapproves."

"I'm sorry," whispered Tina.

"As you know, I'm quite considerably older than Jeremy. He is heavily in debt, with no prospect of digging his way out, either by work or by economising. My father, not entirely unreasonably, thinks that he's marrying me for my money and the kind of help to his career at the Bar that he might expect from a father-in-law with the most prestigious law practice in the country. Isn't that the way you see it, Tina —isn't that the way everyone's going to see it?"

There was no point in beating about the bush with this very formidable woman. Tina nodded. "Yes, I suppose it is."

"And that, having come to the threshold of my forties without having found a man who'll have me, I'm buying myself a personable young man down on his luck. Oh yes, Tina, I have a fortune of my own, left me by my mother. Enough to pay off Jeremy's debts and keep us both in affluence."

Uncomfortable under the challenging stare of those lustrous dark eyes, Tina shrugged and—the hell with tact— asked: "So—what's your problem, Jessica?"

"My problem," said Jessica Rothstein, getting to her feet and moving with pantherene strides across the room, "is that I think Jeremy doesn't love me the way I would wish to be loved." She whirled round and faced the other. "And that's what *you* think too, isn't it?"

"My God, you don't mince words, do you?" replied Tina.

"Answer me—please."

"You want it straight—or wrapped up?" An unnecessary question, but it bought a little time.

"The way you know I want it."

"Okay," said Tina. "If you're yearning for hearts and flowers, you've picked the wrong man. If, on the other hand, you're looking for a man who'll stand by his vows, and honour, defend, and respect you—no more than that; I wouldn't sell Jeremy Cook any higher than that—you've already got him."

Jessica Rothstein smiled—brilliantly and with great heart. "Thanks, Tina," she said. "That's just what I wanted to hear, and I wanted to hear it from you.

"I'm going to go through with this marriage, and do you know why? Because I love the boy. And what you've just told me squares with what I'd already figured out myself: he may have picked me for a meal ticket, but he won't let me down. There's a certain—basic integrity behind that playboy image he presents to the world. And he works hard as well as playing hard, did you know that? He'll work all night on a brief just for the sake of getting it right—thank God for his healthy constitution." She picked up her gloves and held out a hand. "Thanks, for seeing me and being so honest, Tina."

"I'll respect your confidences, Jessica," said Tina.

"Don't you do any such thing!" cried the other, appalled. "Tell 'em all! Tell the world that Jessica Rothstein's marrying for love, and to watch this space in five years' time. We'll have the last laugh yet."

"I think you will, Jessica," said Tina, and meant it.

She saw her visitor out, and watched through the window to see her tall figure striding purposefully towards the King's Road.

"Miss Rothstein," she said aloud. "I take my hat off to you —you really are quite a gal!"

"Ah—good morning, Norman."

"Good morning, ma'am. Where is it to be today?"

"I think I should like a drive to Hampstead, said Miss Tewson. "Hampstead has very happy memories for me."

"Hampstead it is." He helped her into the back seat of the vintage Daimler limousine, arranged a plaid rug across her knees.

"Warm enough, ma'am?" he asked. "There being no heater in the car, like."

She smiled. "My father didn't approve of car heaters," she

said. "He was one of the pioneer motorists in his youth. Regarded car heaters as effete."

"Sounds like a man after my own heart, ma'am. Tough."

"Oh, he was, he was—tough as nails."

Beautifully responsive to the slightest touch of the controls, the old Daimler purred steadily round the outer circle of Regent's Park, where children were flying kites in the blustery wind, and out past the London mosque into the scudding traffic of Park Road.

"Anywhere particular in Hampstead, ma'am?" asked Norman, having slid aside the panel in the glass partition that separated the chauffeur from the passengers.

"Oh, drive around the nice parts and then go up on to the Heath," said Miss Tewson. "There's a rather splendid public house—I don't remember its name—where my father and I used to drive to on Sunday mornings to meet the members of his motoring club. Sometimes we'd go in the Le Mans Aston Martin, all wrapped up and wearing goggles, haha. Sometimes we'd take the *gran turismo* Alfa if we felt rather posh. Ah, those far-off days!"

Through devious ways and secret streets, past gardens behind old walls and dreaming plane trees, they came at length to the broad heath, where the wind combed the grass like unruly hair.

"That's the pub," said Miss Tewson. "And the yard in front where the members used to line up their cars so proudly, wheel to wheel. I wonder—do you know?—I should like to go in and have a hot toddy."

He looked round at her. "I wouldn't advise, ma'am," he said. "It's very cold out there, and you'd have a long walk to the door. Besides, they won't be open yet."

"Ah yes—I hadn't thought of that," said Miss Tewson. "And you're quite right—I do feel the cold very badly these days."

"How do you heat your place, ma'am?" he asked, quickening the car's pace, so that the public house slipped away behind them.

"Central heating. It's very convenient. All Mrs. Everey has to do when she comes in daily is to adjust the knob to suit the weather."

"Never did fancy central heating," said Norman. "Give me a coal fire every time."

"Oh yes," she said with feeling. "But I haven't had one since my father died and all the servants left."

After a while, he said: "See here, ma'am, why don't I take you back and build you a really nice fire? There's plenty of what they call that smokeless solid fuel in the mews."

"Oh yes, that would be lovely," said Miss Tewson. "In the small sitting room. It used to get beautifully warm and cosy in the small sitting room. On winter afternoons, Father and I used to have a heaped-up fire in there, so that one's cheeks glowed, and I would toast crumpets for tea, and we would listen to the wireless . . ."

Norman met his eye in the rear view mirror, and he winked at it.

"You're in, mate," he said half aloud.

Tina had spent the morning at the TV studio on a recording session of two shows which would see her through to the end of the present series, after which there would be another contract—undoubtedly on even more advantageous terms. They had started work at seven, and all she had had since breakfast was a cup of coffee. She felt completely wrung out by the time she got home.

"Tina—oh, thank heaven!" Maggie looked at her wits' end. "I just had this call from Scotland!"

"Jock!"

"He's been arrested!"

"Not *again!*" In the latter days of their marriage, Jock had played many starring roles in the police courts of the land, charged with everything from "drunk and disorderly" to "attempting to obtain credit by false pretences." "What's he done now?"

"They've got him for assault with intent to cause grievous

bodily harm," said Maggie, referring to her note pad. "The guy who rang up was a solicitor. He said bail had been set for two thousand pounds and Jock can be released as soon as the money's been paid into the court—which can be done by hand or by post any time between 10 A.M. and 5 P.M., Saturdays and Sundays excepted."

"But, Maggie—tomorrow's Saturday. That means he'll be locked up in a police cell all over the weekend till the cheque arrives there on Monday morning—even if they'll accept a cheque without some back-up. I couldn't let that happen to anyone—not even to Jock."

"I could fly up to Scotland on the next plane and be there before they close this afternoon," said the other.

Tina looked at her in heartfelt relief. "Oh, Maggie, would you? You're a gem. I'd go myself, but I really couldn't face him. Jock, I mean."

The issue having been settled, Maggie was as excited as a schoolgirl off on an outing to the seaside. "I've never been to Scotland before," she said, thumbing through the flight timetables. "I think I'll make a weekend of it."

"Take till the middle of next week," said Tina. "Things are pretty quiet as far as the office is concerned. Why not?"

"Oh, how super! Gosh, thanks, Tina." Maggie addressed herself to the timetables again. "Here we are—Heathrow to Edinburgh, Turnhouse—there's a flight at two-ten. And it gets me in well on time."

While Maggie went upstairs to pack a suitcase, Tina wrote a cheque for two thousand and left the name of the payee blank for Maggie to fill in. It then occurred to her to ring her bank manager and ask him to facilitate any phone enquiries that might follow the presentation of the cheque; whatever happened, that stupid ex-husband of hers could not be allowed to languish behind bars over the weekend. Jock, for all his faults, was a free spirit, a thing of air and fire: to imprison such a creature would be like caging a skylark.

Maggie came downstairs carrying a suitcase. She was dressed in slacks and a fisherman's knit sweater.

"Where and to whom did Jock carry out this assault with intent to et cetera?" asked Tina.

"The solicitor did say—I don't remember the name without my notes, but it was against some guy in the offices of an offshore oil rig company."

"Ah—another big deal bites the dust!"

"What did you say, Tina?"

"It's nothing. Have a good flight, Maggie. And please phone me when it's all settled."

"Thanks—'bye."

It was only after she had gone that Tina got around to looking for the morning's mail. This was on Maggie's desk, most of it opened and dealt with, the private stuff unopened in a neat pile; in the flak over Jock, Maggie had forgotten to give them to her.

There was a letter from an old medical school friend, an invitation to a party, a brief note from Janet Barden giving the date of the hearing before the Committee a week hence. And a missive from Jamie Farrell:

Dear T.M.

Afraid I got rather drunk and shot my mouth off a bit at that party. Not much of a party.

If you're at a loose end on Sunday, why not come up and we'll take a bird out over the fields as see if we can make a kill. If you're not too squeamish, that is. Come in the afternoon.

Yours,
    J.F.

(There follows the transcript of a tape recording taken from a telephone conversation between Mr. David Carruthers and his stepmother, Mrs. Iris Carruthers, which was contrived by the former—quote—'In case there was any subsequent dispute.')

IC: Hello? . . .
DC: Hello, Iris dear. It's David.

IC: Uh!—hello.

DC: Are you well, Iris?

IC: Well as can be expected, I s'pose. Don't often have the honour of a call from you. Must be important.

DC: Well, you know—just ringing to see if you're okay, all alone there in that big house.

IC: I know you'd like to shovel me off into some slum hovel in the country, so's you and your brood can come and lord it in my husband's house.

DC: Don't let's fall out about that again, Iris. I've told you again and again, you're perfectly entitled—and welcome—to stay at the Grange until—well . . .

IC: Until I snuff it? Very nicely put, I'm sure.

(A pause)

DC: However, that wasn't what I rang about, Iris. What I rang about was this withdrawal of five thousand pounds you propose to make.

IC: *(suspiciously)* How do you know about that—you been snooping on me again?

DC: Now, Iris, you know very well that under the terms of my father's will, I'm empowered . . .

IC: You're a born snooper, David Carruthers! Why, when you were a brat and I married your father, you used to listen at our bedroom door. That's a snooper for you!

(A pause)

DC: Iris, let's be reasonable. I'm only doing this for your own good. If you'll just put me in the picture as to why you need this quite considerable sum of money. Is it, perhaps, for repairs to the house?

(Pause)

DC: No, it couldn't be that. The estate looks after all expenditure on the Grange. Are you, perhaps, planning to take a long holiday?

IC: A holiday—yes!

DC: Well, that settles it, doesn't it? Er—this sounds like a

pretty expensive holiday if you have to pay out five
thousand in advance. Is it—a world cruise?

IC: Yes, a world cruise. I've always wanted to go on a
world cruise. And now I'm going.

DC: Good for you, Iris, good for you. Um—which ship-
ping line are you travelling with, Iris?

IC: I don't know.

DC: But you *must* know, Iris. If you've received an in-
voice for your fare in advance, it will be clearly set
out—the name of the company and the name of the
ship. What ship are you sailing in, Iris?

IC: You're trying to trap me, aren't you? That's what
you're trying to do—*trap me!*

DC: Iris, I . . .

IC: Well, you're wasting your time, you dirty little
snooper! I'm not going to listen to you anymore—
but just you listen to me—I shall be round there at
the bank just as soon as the doors open. And I shall
demand my money—in cash!

DC: In—*cash?* . . .

(Sound of the receiver being slammed down at the other end)

DC: Iris—*Iris!* . . .

*(An attempt is made to repeat the call, but the phone is not an-
swered.)*

EIGHT

Sunday morning it rained, and Tina, who had hired a car on the off chance that she might firmly make up her mind, found herself quite unexpectedly disappointed, since she thought she remembered Jamie Farrell saying that he never flew hawks in teeming rain. By midday, however, the sun came out, the sky dried, and the pavement on the sunny side of Lochiel Street was soon steaming merrily. She got herself an early lunch of cold meat and salad with a glass of milk, and was heading east by half-past twelve.

She was in good mood. Maggie had rung at about seven on the Friday evening. All fixed: she had arrived at the court in good time, and the clerk had accepted without demur the cheque from the famous TV personality Dr. Tina. Jock, relieved at his reprieve, had taken her out for a drink. No, he was not to be drawn on the circumstances of the alleged offence, but seemed quite chirpy. She—Maggie—was checking in at a hotel in Princes Street, Edinburgh, and planning a riotous weekend of sightseeing. Back midweek.

The last of London petered out north of Hackney marshes, and semi-rural Essex took over. Tina found herself anticipating her forthcoming encounter with Farrell with a certain ambivalence: on the one hand he still retained the undeniable attraction that had struck her so forcibly when she first saw him expounding his arcane art on TV; offset against that there was his sullen waywardness, his seeming determination to make himself thoroughly dislikeable. Taking one thing with another, she supposed that she had always had a soft spot for self-determining eccentrics. Johnny Kettle had been almost the archetypal eccentric—save that, unlike Farrell, his eccentricity had been of the kind that one could have warmed one's hands against, with no sharp edges of self-doubt; only loving and giving, and a certain taste for irony that sharpened the blandness like a piquant sauce.

She came presently to the lane that wound down to Farrell's thatched cottage. He must have heard her approach, for he was waiting for her.

"Glad you're sensibly dressed," he said. "The fields are still wet and we might have a bit of wading to do if the gos decides to take to the trees beyond the stream."

Tina, mindful of the changeable weather, had come along in jeans and wellingtons, a thick jersey, waterproof jacket, and beret.

"How are you?" she asked, being determined not to let his overbearingness trample all over common civility.

"Well enough," he answered carelessly. "Come on."

He had with him a lurcher dog that Tina had not seen before. He seemed quite friendly in a guarded sort of way; she supposed he did not get a lot of affection—but seemed content enough to nuzzle Tina's proffered hand.

"Don't make a fool of that damned dog," was Farrell's comment.

The line of predatory birds was strung across the back lawn on perches. "We'll take the intermewed goshawk," said her companion. "And while we're about it, I'll give you a running commentary by way of a lesson.

"Gear: this is your hawking bag. In it you carry everything you need to meet any emergency in the field: some tempting grub in the form of a piece of shin of beef—this is in case all else fails and your hawk persists in sitting up there in a treetop instead of returning to the fist on call. If this fails, you've got your lure—and that's the thing which you saw in my first little demonstration: you whirl it round and round, and the hawk's lured into the belief that it's a live prey.

"Bits and pieces: a whistle, because this particular gos has been trained to come to the whistle as well as the voice. Spare bits and pieces of leather gear, a spare swivel. And a good length of cord. Last of all, a decent pair of binoculars—just in case you lose your hawk in a big way and have to go searching. Right—off we go."

Tina watched, fascinated, as he approached the goshawk, whose beady yellow eyes fixed unblinkingly upon her master, who kept his gloved right hand behind his back.

"See how she sits quite calmly?" said Farrell. "Head slightly forward. Keen, but not silly keen. I don't want her to leap out at me and wet her primary wing feathers on the damp grass. "Come on, then. Good girl!"

With a jingle of the bells attached to each ankle, the goshawk made a wing-assisted hop and landed fair and square upon the proffered gauntlet, and Farrell secured her by binding her leash around his palm and fingers. "Now we're in business," he said. He grinned fiercely at Tina. "The killing business," he added.

They traversed the paddock, Farrell leading, with Tina walking a few paces behind him, on his right flank, so that she could see the goshawk, whose bright-eyed, hook-beaked profile was forever flicking from one view to another, alert to the slightest movement: a wind-blown spear of meadow grass, the shadow of a passing cloud, Tina—when she stumbled slightly over a tussock. And the lurcher, whose name turned out to be Jim, searched the grass twenty yards ahead of their advance, darting to and fro on a front of about ten yards, nose to the ground, sometimes retracing his tracks when he had second thoughts about a scent.

Beyond the paddock, they passed through a five-barred gate and into a meadow that undulated down to a fast-flowing stream in a shallow valley, to rise up again for about half a mile, where a line of poplar marked the far hedgerow.

Farrell veered his direction of advance to approach the stream at an acute angle, whistling and gesturing to the lurcher similarly to amend his line of progress.

Ignorant of the likely outcome of the manoeuvre, Tina let her mind wander to the contemplation of the scenery about her: the broad meadowlands stretching to the north and east as far as an horizon of blue-green and indeterminate grey-ness. Very John Constable, the massive cloud formations, also. High and to her left, far off, a V-formation of wild geese headed eastwards towards the marshy Essex coast. The gos-hawk saw them also and tensed herself for an instant before returning to the untiring search of her immediate surround-ings.

And then—the peace and quiet fell apart . . .

Jim the lurcher stopped in his tracks, one paw still raised in mid-stride.

"He's got a scent!" breathed Farrell.

Next instant, a bounding, dun-brown form appeared from out of nowhere a yard in front of the lurcher's nose.

"Leave it, Jim!" shouted Farrell. "Still, boy! Lie, damn you!"

And he released the hawk, helping her on her way with a forward sweep of his gauntleted hand. The lurcher stayed put.

By this time, the prey—it was a sizeable hare—had cov-ered at least fifty yards from its standing start, and at its best turn of speed. Add this to the distance from the falconer to the spot where the lurcher had disturbed it, and it seemed to the unpractised eye that the goshawk would have her work cut out to overtake the speeding quarry.

As Tina was to observe, nothing could have been further from the truth . . .

Flying low, the predator fixed herself upon the loping form ahead and streaked in to the attack. Closing fast, she gained height as if to make a pounce. Tina held her breath.

"Watch closely," muttered Farrell at her elbow. "This will be good! Watch the hare when the gos makes a stoop to kill!" The enjoinder was quite unnecessary: riveted by an awe-some fascination that teetered on the edge of something much more unpleasant, Tina could not have dragged her gaze away for worlds.

The goshawk was now above and slightly behind the hare.

Suddenly, she closed her wings and fell like a stone. An instant later, she was sprawled awkwardly in the ground, wings and tail feathers splayed, with a foolish, open-beaked expression on her angry face. And the hare, who had turned in its own length an instant before the cruel talons would have closed upon it, was streaking off at a tangent.

Farrell laughed. "Ha! That'll teach her that life isn't all beer and skittles!" he roared.

Tina, who was experiencing an almost physical sense of relief and release, said nothing.

"The gos has got her dander up," declared Farrell, "there'll be no checking her now. Watch how she goes."

The hawk was airborne again and once more in hot pursuit. The hare, having been successful with its first evasion, redoubled its efforts to shake off the attacker, or at least to baulk the hawk's attempts to strike; jinking from side to side, turning about on itself, making sudden stops and starts, it had the wheeling goshawk in some confusion—but still she remained substantially above her prey, and never far from a position of attack. Both creatures, each master of its own element, displayed a like grace, skill and cunning; but Tina May had firmly decided where her own allegiance lay.

Let the hare get away, she whispered to herself. Please— *please!* . . .

She was slow to appreciate the finer points of the next figure in that elegant dance of death, though Farrell undoubtedly perceived it and was sporting a tight-lipped, narrow-eyed grin.

"The gos has him!" he muttered. "It's only a matter of time now. The cunning jade!"

The fact was that the goshawk was concentrating her pressure upon the intended victim from the upper part of the slope down to the stream, and the main direction of the hare's evasions was being inclined slowly but constantly towards the water. The full realisation of this struck the fugitive when, having made a particularly sharp turn, it found the way ahead barred along its whole front.

And then—it began to scream . . .

Tina, who had never before heard the despairing scream of a cornered hare, was shocked, and instinctively turned to Farrell for a reflection of the horror that must be showing in her own expression; instead, she saw a countenance enrapt with a savage joy and triumph. She watched him, all unbelieving, while the hare continued its thin, shrill, strangled scream (it has been likened to the panic cry of an old man in mortal fear), agonisingly aware of the yawning gulf that lay between them.

"Now, gos, is your chance!" gritted the falconer.

Gone the wide expanse of the open field. Hemmed in against the fast-flowing stream, the hare's options had been circumscribed by one quarter; furthermore, it was tiring of its frantic efforts, while the goshawk, moving as she was in a vastly easier element, and controlling her movements by only the lightest touches of wings and tail, was as keen and lively as the instant she had been entered into the encounter. And she sensed—knew—that the hare was nearly finished.

The end, when it came, was a repeat of the first stoop to kill—only this time the goshawk landed fair and square on the hare's shoulders and her talons—sharp and curved as eight cavalry sabres and each with the power of a steel vise—were driven deeply through skin and muscle, vein and artery, to bone.

Farrell started to run, and Tina followed after him, hopeful against all likelihood that, the sporting chase over, the falconer was going to rescue the hare.

The goshawk was not having an easy ride. Clamped to her victim, she was being thrown all ways by her leaping, bucking mount—but she hung on while her victim entered into the final, wild figure of the death dance, screaming all the while and jetting fine streams of veinous and arterial blood from its multiple wounds.

"Stop it, stop it!" cried Tina. "Please—*please!*"

"No problem!" grinned Farrell savagely, as, stooping, he gathered up the hawk in his right, gloved hand—and she sprang to his fist quite readily, since he had garnished it with the piece of raw beef—whilst with the other he took the wounded hare by the throat, gave a sharp wrench, and broke the neck.

Tina gasped in horror.

He looked up at her with vicious contempt.

"Spare me your shrinking squeamishness!" he shouted. "This is where mercy and compassion enter into nature's equation of life and death. That's the way it really is—*corpse doctor!*"

She recoiled from him; turned on her heel and fled up the slope, running as hard as she was able—anywhere—anywhere to shut out the vile abuse that he threw after her:

"You can't face up to the fact of mortality, you mealy-mouthed moral virgin! I've met your sort—you're the kind who'd set a broken leg on a sewer rat, or keep a child dying by inches on a life support machine! Anything but soil your precious fingers with the business of dying! The very process disgusts you—you're only at home with the end of the production line—*a nice safe corpse!*"

She could still hear him when, having traversed the meadow and crossed the paddock, she raced round the cottage, breath labouring and her heart drumming, and threw herself into the car.

Then she was away down the lane, crashing every gear in her wild haste to place as much distance as soon as possible between herself and everything connected with Jamie Farrell, his works, and his philosophy.

Tina found herself still shaking when she arrived home. The hand that directed the Scotch bottle that half filled the tumbler was badly out of control, and when she sloshed water into it direct from the kitchen faucet, a large part of the mixture went into the sink.

She eased herself down into the comfortable basket chair, tucked her stockinged feet under her, and huddled with the glass clutched in both hands, shivering with emotion and sucking in the diluted spirit like a child at its drinking bottle.

Everything passes. Within half an hour of quiet, she had gained control over herself again and was ruefully contemplating how in the world she had managed the mechanics of driving back down from Essex and right across London to Chelsea. Her good fairy must have been co-driving—and thank heaven for Sunday and the empty roads.

Another stiff Scotch poured and taken in a more civilised manner, and she had recovered from the shock of that hideous episode. By the time the shadows had lengthened right across Lochiel Street and she was sitting in the unlit gloom, her thoughts had directed her to a course of action which, though its motivation was still obscure to her and the possible outcome unlikely of any firm resolvement, nevertheless had to be followed—if only to exorcise the demon that had sprung up—whole, alive, and screaming for answers—in her mind.

Contingent upon this, she telephoned Tony Dacres and, employing what private enquiry agents euphemistically describe as a plausible pretext, requested of him a name and an address or phone number. A little small talk, an exchange of compliments, and she rang off and made a second connection: this time to fix an appointment for the following morning.

The house was in Devonshire Place, which lies within the enclave bounded by Portland Place, Wigmore Street, Marylebone Road, and its High Street, thus entitling the occupier to describe himself as having a Harley Street practice.

In fact, Stuart Preece shared the house with eight other practitioners, two to a floor. A word in the entry phone gave Tina admission, and she was presently ushered into a suave consulting room decorated in jasper green with white mouldings, where a half-familiar figure rose from behind a Georgian desk to greet her.

"Dr. May, this is a pleasure. We never even got around to

being introduced at Tony's party. Incidentally, tell it not in Gath, but it was far from the social event of the season, was it?"

"For me it was quite awful," said Tina. "Tony had a gobbet of ill news that, taken alone, would have quite ruined my evening."

When she was seated comfortably before him, he smiled over his folded hands at her. As she had remembered him, Preece was youngish—now in his late thirties—dark, saturnine, attractive—and knew it.

"Now," he said by way of starters. "You were very mysterious when you rang me. Said it was a very important personal matter, and that you couldn't speak of it over the telephone. I was most intrigued—and still am."

"It's very good of you to see me at such short notice," said Tina.

He shrugged, smiling. "In our calling, it behoves us to stick together and help each other," he declared. "In this world of TV and enlightened semi-literacy for all, we have forfeited much of the mystique we once enjoyed. It follows that we must close ranks against a sceptical world.

"Now—how can I help you?"

Tina took a deep breath. "It concerns—Jamie Farrell," she said.

He frowned reflectively. "Jamie—Farrell? Do I? . . ."

"You talked to him at Tony's party," she prompted. "Most of the evening," she added.

"Aaaah!" His expression changed. Hardened.

"Yes, you remember him now," said Tina. "You formed a certain—opinion about him. I have to tell you, Mr. Preece, that I was an unwitting eavesdropper to that opinion."

"And he's a friend of yours?" asked Preece. "I think I see it all."

"No, I don't think you do."

He cocked an ironic eyebrow. "Then I'm not to be sued for libel?"

"Far from it. I want to ask you to expand upon your remark."

"Why—what's your interest? If I may ask. Are you perhaps —involved with this man?"

"As a friend, merely. And I'm not so sure that we're friends any longer. Let's say my interest is higher than common curiosity, but less than concerned involvement. Does that answer your question?"

"It'll suffice," said Preece. He settled himself back in his chair and, folding his hands across his spare middle, looked across at Tina, head on one side, suddenly very serious. "You must realise, before I begin, that friend Farrell had been knocking back champagne cocktails like there was no tomorrow, and the present speaker didn't trust himself to drive home that night.

"So much for the background. Notwithstanding his condition, I formed the opinion that Farrell was to some degree insane—and remarked as much to Tony Dacres—and that, I suppose, is what you overheard."

She nodded. "Tell me why you formed this opinion."

"Well," said Preece, "he dictated the conversation from the first by introducing the topic of terminal illness. Did you say something, Dr. May?"

"It was nothing," replied Tina.

"He posed the notion that surely I, as a brain surgeon, must see many such cases. I responded by hinting at some of the truly tragic examples that have passed through my hands. And he seemed to get very excited: started to extol the virtues of euthanasia, about which, as you know, there's been a lot of controversial claptrap broadcasted recently. Wanted to know my views. Well, I gave him the conventional, middle-of-the-road summation that most of us share in the profession: that negative euthanasia in the shape of switching off life-support machines in hopeless cases, not treating the old man's friend pneumonia, and so forth is perfectly justified in certain circumstances.

"He listened to my spiel with mounting impatience—and

then broke in with a demand to know where I stood on positive euthanasia. Of course, I told him I didn't stand anywhere—that it was suspect, dangerous morally, socially, and in every other way. And open to the wildest abuse."

"How did he react to that?" asked Tina.

"He went bananas. Accused me of everything from cowardice to moral turpitude, with flagrant hypocrisy for good measure. It was then I formed the opinion that he was unbalanced. After he'd said his piece, he seemed to calm down for a bit, and even half apologised. I responded by sort of temporising; put it to him that I respected his point of view but that, as a member of the medical profession, I was obliged to follow certain rules of professional conduct. He listened with some interest and seemed to appreciate my offering of the olive branch. He even calmed down. And then he asked me—quite casually—if I had any terminal cases on my hands at the moment. Like a fool, instead of tactfully changing the subject, I admitted that I had such a one, and without particularising, gave a general prognosis, which happens to be pretty shattering.

"Bang! He was right back with the staring eyes and the gibberish. Would I give him the patient's name and address? Why? Because he'd visit the patient, persuade him to make an end of himself! And this is the part that opened my eyes to friend Farrell: he said he'd willingly help the patient out of his misery by assisting him to do away with himself!"

Tina drew a deep, shuddering breath. "I see," she murmured.

"Mind you," said Preece, "I speak only as a brain surgeon when I say that he's insane. To confirm that, you'd need a psychiatrist. They're the chaps who pass judgement on the fine adjustments of the mind; we're merely the manual workers who chop bits off here and there. Tell the story to a good psychiatrist—see what he thinks."

"I'll do that, Mr. Preece," promised Tina.

It was a busy day for Derek Arkwright, whose mother kept house for him in Norbury. Mrs. Arkwright had suffered quite a bad fall that morning and broken her hip. He had spent an hour or so with her at the hospital before racing up to the Yard to attend the weekly review conference of senior officers. Eschewing lunch, he was back in his office at one o'clock to make some inroads upon the stuff piled up on his desk. His secretary WPC Joyce Treece was eager to be helpful:

"I'll stay and give you a hand, Mr. Arkwright."

"Not to worry, Joy, I'll cope. Hop off and have your lunch —but bring me up a ham sandwich and coffee when you've finished, please."

It was then that Turner broke in with scant ceremony.

"Sir, we have another candidate for the syndrome!" he announced with triumph. "And it's been under our noses for days. It was computer who winkled it out."

"It's a wonder that murders were ever solved before computers were invented," observed Arkwright. "Tell me all about it."

"Mrs. Alice Pouter," read Turner from a clipboard. "Widow lady of Harrow. Murdered by breaking of neck that must have called for considerable strength and skill"—he looked up—"the Harrow police surgeon who performed the P.M. suggested that the murderer might well be in that line, and suggested we look out for an all-in wrestler."

"Sounds an intelligent guess. Go on."

"Like I said, sir, it slipped through our fingers, and that was because of the *modus operandi.* However—there was a large sum of money involved—and it's gone missing."

"How much?"

"Two grand. Drawn out in cash the day before Mrs. Pouter was murdered."

"That puts Mrs. Pouter in the syndrome as far as I'm concerned," declared Arkwright.

"Computer agrees, sir," said Turner.

"The sample having been increased by one on the issue of

the missing money, I think we're going to have to reconsider Tostig."

"Yes, sir," said Turner. "That's what computer thinks, too."

"I'm so glad that we're managing to keep up with the little dear!" said Arkwright acidly.

NINE

That afternoon, again by hurried appointment, Tina May called at a nursing home in a quiet square off Wigmore Street. A matron with a faintly disapproving air led her down discreet, pine-smelling corridors to the director's office which bore the legend: DOCTOR D. C. HEYMANS.

"Dr. May to see you, Doctor," said the matron severely, glowering at Tina as she went in.

The director bounded to his feet: a stocky figure in a double-breasted suit with a red silk handkerchief fluttering foppishly from the top pocket. Tina remembered him instantly from the one occasion when they had met—a Scotland Yard conference at which Heymans had attended to give a psychiatrist's view. Director of this top psychiatric nursing home, writer of popular bestsellers on everything from Love and Marriage to Sex for Teenagers, he had once cornered for himself a useful market in his own field on television that was only eclipsed and finally crowded out by Johnny Kettle's programme. If Heymans felt any resentment on this score he had not shown it at their previous meeting—nor did he now.

"My dear Dr. May, how very, *very* nice to see you again," he cried, rushing round his desk to seize her hand and implant a kiss upon it. "You're looking tremendously well, and as beautiful as ever!" To the visibly affronted matron, he said: "My dear, send our little Nurse Summers along with some tea, if you would be so kind."

The matron sniffed and left. Dr. Heymans rubbed his hands gleefully and sat down. "A nice cup of tea will set us up for our deliberations, my dear," he said. He glanced archly at Tina and chuckled. "Though I confess to being a little puzzled as to why you wanted to see me so urgently." He switched facial masks from comedy to tragedy. "I hope the matter is not—*grave*," he added.

"Not in the least," lied Tina. "And I wonder at my presumption. I'm looking to you for help in the presentation of one of my TV cases."

"Are you now, young lady—are you," said Heymans, and showed his reaction by sinking low in his chair, hands in pockets, sulky-eyed.

"It concerns a point of psychiatric verisimilitude."

"It would, wouldn't it?" growled Heymans. He sank his chin against his chest and glowered at his visitor.

"Though a forensic pathologist," said Tina, "I do occasionally come into indirect contact with mental illnesses and am always at a loss. What I need is an absolute top person in the field to whom I can turn in an emergency. And, naturally, Dr. Heymans—I thought of you."

Heymans hitched his trouser knees and perched his neat, crocodile-shod feet on the corner of the desk. "I like your approach, my dear," he said. "It's pleasantly oblique. Perhaps, after all, I may be able to advise you." He twinkled a smile. "Tell me your problem."

The feminine click-click of heels in the corridor outside announced the approach of Nurse Summers with the tea. She was in white and mauve and was most extraordinarily pretty. Dr. Heymans fussed around her, patting her shoulder as she laid the tray upon his desk, and followed her with his eyes all the way to the door. Tina felt like a voyeur.

"And now," said Heymans, pouring tea, "the problem . . ."

"The problem," repeated Tina, reaching to take the proffered cup and saucer. She then gave him what she described as an outline of an imaginary character, omitting—for the sake of concealing Farrell's identity—that he was a falconer, but stressing instead his detached, not to say casual, attitude to animal suffering and death.

Recounting as through a third party, she next gave Heymans the substance of the conversation between Farrell and Preece, more or less as she had heard it from the latter. Heymans listened throughout with no interruption save a nodding of his head—as if in tacit approbation.

"You'll appreciate, of course, Dr. . . ."

"Dermot," he prompted her. "If we are to be collaborators, my dear Tina, you must from now on address me as Dermot."

Tina nodded. "Very well, Dermot. As I was saying, you'll realise that the cases I portray on TV bear only coincidental resemblances to actual persons—as the phrase goes."

"Quite, quite," said the other, nodding.

"But I like to get my facts—clinical, analytical, diagnostic, and so forth—as nearly accurate as possible. Most of the time I think I get pretty close . . ."

"Oh, you do, you do—I watch all your programmes," Heymans assured her.

"Now, I have to tell you that, despite the disclaimer, the person I have described is loosely based on a living character."

"I had thought as much," said Heymans. "It rang so true."

"Well then," said Tina. "Speaking as a psychiatrist, can you, from the slender outline I've given you, go out on a limb and diagnose this man's mental state? Is he, or is he not, insane?"

"He is as sane as you or I," came the response.

"Oh!"

"You look—and sound—disappointed, my dear Tina."

"Not disappointed, not by any means," she replied. "It's just that I can't imagine a sane person contemplating—what he is contemplating. And may, indeed, have already carried out," she added.

Heymans drained his teacup, assumed his former attitude of feet on the desk, and switched expression to indulgent avuncular.

"My dear Tina, loose expressions like sanity and insanity

(together with such concepts of the McNaghten Rules—one of my *bêtes noires,* against which I rail on every convenient occasion), simply do not take into account the wide, grey swath of irrational human behaviour that lies between those two convenient terms implying white and black. And if you are in any doubt on that score, read Freud on psychopathology in everyday life.

"Your Mr. Anon undoubtedly inhabits that grey area, and has probably done so since childhood. Possibly an under-achiever—though it would scarcely make any difference, for he has never made his mark as he would have wished, and consequently suffers from a sense of inferiority which manifests itself in sullenness, gaucherie, and mildly antisocial behaviour occasionally illuminated by flashes of conscious charm. As a consolation, he possibly possesses a competence in a sort of activity that brings little or no popular acclaim or financial benefit. Does that sound like your Mr. Anon, Tina?"

"Uncannily so," she replied.

"Well, now, where do we go from here?" said Heymans, tapping his fingertips together and putting on a judicial face. "We have it from a third party that he is committed to the theory—and possibly the practise—of positive euthanasia. Yes, I think that would be entirely in his character: the sense of inferiority, his falling short of his own standard of achievement. A control over life and death—that would very adequately compensate for all these. He would become—like a god, a dispenser of easeful death."

"But—he speaks of it in terms of mercy and compassion," interposed Tina.

"Undoubtedly," retorted Heymans. "The godlike illusion is for his ego only, and he scarcely acknowledges it even to his conscious self. The conventional expressions of mercy and compassion—they are for external consumption."

"Is he—dangerous?" asked Tina.

"Yes," replied the other. "Given certain circumstances—as, for instance, if someone attempted to thwart his compul-

sion towards positive euthanasia—he could be very dangerous.''

"One thing more," said Tina. "These—victims of positive
euthanasia, whether willing or unwilling. Would he, in any
circumstances, take money from them, or even steal money
from them?"

"Not for his own benefit," said Heymans without hesita-
tion. "Gods are above filthy lucre. But, say, if the enterprise
called for some degree of financial support that he couldn't
sustain, he would think it perfectly in order to pass the plate
round—like they do in church." He laughed, and almost
immediately cut it short and assumed a pious face.

They parted at his front door, to which he had escorted
her, with the matron glowering in the background.

He kissed her hand. "Till our next meeting, Tina," he said
with a smouldering glance.

"And thank you for your help, Dermot," she replied.

"A word of warning," he said. "Be careful."

"Yes, I will."

The next showing of "The Pathologist" was at peak time
on the following evening, Tuesday. First checking by phone
that Elles was around, Tina took a cab to the studio and told
his secretary that she must see him on a matter of life and
death, thereby employing a considerable amount of overkill,
for producers of high-rated shows will wade through treacle
at the behest of their stars; it is only when the ratings begin
to sag that small indicators start to raise their ugly heads, in
manifestations such as: "The producer's on the other line,"
or "He's in conference," or "Just take a seat and he'll be
right along when he's free"—things like that.

Elles was round at his office before Tina had scarcely been
made comfortable in the best seat and his secretary had
poured her a gin and tonic.

"Tina darling, what a lovely surprise. Can I take you out to
dinner?"

"Thanks, Simon," she said, "but this isn't a social visit. I came about tomorrow night's programme."

"So where's the problem, Tina?" he asked. "We have two shows in the can, both excellent. If you've any preference for their running order, Tina, you only have to say the word . . .

Elles was anxious, and looked it; in such a manner does the slightest hint of a shadow crossing the star's face excite a producer's ulcer.

"I would like to put on another programme entirely, Simon," she replied. Tina never used the term "show" in connection with "The Pathologist." "And I'd like it to go out live."

"A-another one? A replacement—and *live?*" Simon Elles, provincial grammar school to Oxford scholarship, had a clear vision of having to sell his villa in Sardinia and take the son of his broken marriage away from Charterhouse. "Live, darling, with a programme so controversial as 'The Pathologist,' is quite out of the question," he said.

"But I must insist," said Tina, without heat.

Goodbye, Sardinia! Elles picked himself up and sought around for a way to compromise with this suddenly implacable version of the easiest star with whom he had ever had to deal.

"This replacement programme—er—what kind of subject or subjects did you have in mind, Tina?" he asked with the earnestness of desperation.

"One subject only," she replied. "Euthanasia."

"It's a very hot topic at the moment," conceded Elles. "A lot of big noises in the medical profession worldwide are publicly owning up to negative euthanasia . . ."

"I have in mind a case of positive euthanasia," said Tina, "and how it is diagnosed through forensic pathology. Strictly between ourselves, Simon, I have—or I think I have —just such a case on my files at this moment."

Elles's creative mind instantly seized upon the concept, enveloped it, and swallowed it whole.

"I like it!" he said. "It's different, and right in the epicentre of current controversy. We'll do it, Tina—we'll record it for next week's programme for sure."

Tina shook her head. "Tomorrow, Simon. I want it to be put out tomorrow night—live."

Thrust back again into square one, the nimble-minded Elles sought to broaden out the argument with a little picador work. "Do you have a script prepared for this subject, Tina?" he asked. "Or an outline, perhaps?" No—he could see from her expression that she hadn't.

"I don't need a script," she said. "The main points of the case have already happened. I shall present them, suitably disguised, changed, wrapped up, straight off the top of my head."

"But—the lines for Jakeman to follow when he comes to interrogating you?" said Elles. "Toby's a great ad-libber, but he needs points of reference, starting points—even if it's only a quick read-through of the script."

"I'll give him plenty of leads on the way through," said Tina. "I'll throw him the cues—then he'll have to drive with the seat of his pants—in your own phrase."

Simon Elles had not gotten where he was by thumping the table and forcing through his own ideas come hell come high water, but by compromise and the exploitation of the possible. In the course of the conversation he had elicited that Tina May was clearly going to stick by her guns and insist on a Tuesday showing of the enthanasia programme. It was well within his writ to approve the plan.

"Okay," he conceded. "Script or no script, we'll have it the way you want it. The replacement programme goes out tomorrow night unscripted. But . . ."

"But? . . ." echoed Tina May.

"Not live," he said. "There are too many scratchy elements in 'The Pathologist' to take the risk of someone pulling the indiscretion of the century. Anyhow, Tina, I couldn't authorise it if I wanted to—and the powers-that-be would turn the notion down flat. What I can offer is a recording with a half-hour moratorium, which gives us time to edit out possible nasties before we go on the air at eight. Do you accept that, Tina?"

"I accept that as being very reasonable, Simon." She smiled.

"Let's drink to that," said Elles with some fervour.

By leaps and bounds, the enterprising Norman had insinuated himself into the shabby elegance of Miss Tewson's York Terrace apartment and into the lonely woman's life.

That evening, seated face-to-face in the small sitting room that overlooked the mews, with a banked-up fire bringing a glow to Miss Tewson's parchment cheeks, they were playing Scrabble.

"You're very good, Norman," she commented. "To develop 'nursery' into 'nurseling' shows not only an agile mind, but also a wide vocabulary. My father was an adept at the game, and gave me many fine tips, till I became no mean player myself." She put down a row of cards.

Norman gave a discreet cough.

"What is it?" demanded Miss Tewson.

"Pardon me, ma'am," said Norman, "but I think you'll find there's no such word as 'grazer.' ''

"Nonsense!" retorted she. "From the word 'graze,' which means to feed cattle in a grass meadow. A farmer might say: 'I am grazing my cattle in this or that meadow.' And he would be a 'grazer'—or a person who grazes cattle."

Norman looked apologetic. "Ma'am, I think the word is 'grazier,' '' he said. "Spelt 'g-r-a-z-*i*-e-r.' ''

"We'll soon settle that!" declared Miss Tewson. "Fetch the Oxford dictionary. It's over there on the bookshelf."

He obeyed, and came back riffling through the pages. Having found what he sought, he laid the volume on the card table before her.

Miss Tewson took up the lorgnette which hung about her neck on a black moiré ribbon and peered through it at the printed page.

"Oh!" she exclaimed presently.

"I'm sorry, ma'am," said Norman.

The hand that lowered the lorgnette seemed to tremble slightly, and a cloud of self-doubt flittered across the Amazonian countenance that had silenced committees innumerable with one steely glance.

"I sometimes think," she murmured brokenly, "that my mind is going. Do you know, Norman, I spent half the morning wondering what had happened to Mrs. Settle, and why she hadn't turned up."

"You told her on Saturday that she needn't come any more, ma'am," was his gentle response. " 'Cos you don't need a daily woman anymore—not now I'm coming in every day, cleaning up for you, doing the shopping and making the fires, taking you for spins in the Daimler."

"Ah yes, you're such a blessing, Norman," she said. "I don't know how I managed before you came. You've bucked me up no end. I only hope that you'll put up with my tiresome little ways." She was very near to tears.

"Don't worry, ma'am," he said. "I know when I'm well off. You're a real lady, and a good boss."

"A good boss!" she smiled crookedly. "Never thought I'd ever hear myself so described."

"I hope I didn't speak out of turn like, ma'am."

"Not at all, not at all, Norman," she assured him. "Glad you're happy to be working for me. And only hope you'll stay."

"Of course I will," he said. "For as long as you want me."

"Thank you, thank you," said Miss Tewson. "That's a great comfort. And you may rest assured that—it will not be for all that much longer. You'll scarcely have time to tire of your—your 'good boss.' "

"Oh, don't say that, ma'am," said Norman. "Why, you're as fit as a . . ." He paused on the brink of a pardonable exaggeration.

"No, I'm very poorly old lady," said Miss Tewson. "I suffer great pain and discomfort, and, till you came, a most terrible loneliness." Her voice clouded. "Sometimes I have thought that, if it weren't for my retaining many of my Christian beliefs, I might have—have ended it all . . ." She bowed her head.

Norman, catching sight of his reflexion in the ornate carved mirror above the chimneypiece, winked broadly to himself and grinned.

Back home alone in Lochiel Street, Tina wished she had accepted Simon Elles's offer of dinner. Her small victory turned to anticlimax, she felt flat and restless, and quite disinclined to the notion of eating a lonely supper and going to bed with a book. Maggie had not rung again, so she supposed that her secretary was enjoying the fleshpots of Edinburgh. Lucky she.

The television promising nothing in the way of interest, and a search of the fridge and deep-freeze disclosing only the ingredients for fry-ups and boring items like cottage pie, she threw on a coat and went out to a little Italian restaurant in the King's Road and then on to a late-night movie featuring a double bill of horror.

Tina sat in the gloom, munching on a chocolate bar and dispassionately regarding scenes of the gory violence which she supposed was an anodyne to the dreary and unfulfilled lives of the masses, and so totally unlike the world of mayhem in whose detritus she spent so much of her own workaday existence. And this line of thought brought her to her motives for forcing the programme about euthanasia . . .

Jamie Farrell was the starting point: the catalyst who had slanted her mind towards the theory that euthanasia might be the background to the Turner syndrome. Farrell was almost certainly made in the image that Heymans had postulated. Whether he had actually practised euthanasia or not was immaterial; he had provided her with a theory—and the makings of a programme which would flesh out that theory and make it comprehensible. She must remember to phone Derek Arkwright and tell him to be sure to watch the programme tomorrow night. He might buy the euthanasia explanation and set in train a whole new line of enquiry.

She only hoped that Jamie Farrell, if he saw the programme, wouldn't run away with the mistaken idea that it was aimed directly at him! She yawned. Time for bed and sleepy at last. She went out, leaving the common man to his gory opiate.

Tina arrived at the studio at five-thirty on Tuesday evening and went straight to make-up, where Susan the make-up girl enthused about the star's not too flouncy print dress with the strong neckline—ideal for close shots, and a challenge to the art of the cosmetician.

"Not that I could go wrong with you, Tina," she said. "With your bone structure, hair, and complexion, you could get away with a dab of powder, period. And, honest, you always look so goddamned healthy—which is half the battle."

"Flatterer," said Tina. "And if I look healthy, it's because I took a holiday today and rested the afternoon through."

Toby Jakeman was in the Hospitality Room and already half-way down his first large Scotch on the rocks. With his florid face and beefy jowls, he looked like an extended caricature of his own self as he turned and fixed Tina with a glare of his protuberant baby-blue eyes.

"Hey, Tina, for Chrissake, what's this about no script for tonight's show?" he demanded. "What are you trying to do —put my wife and kids out onto the street?"

"You'll do fine, Toby," she assured him. "I'll lay the ground bait after you've given me the standard build-up and lead-in. And I'll hand you cues and talking points on silver platters."

The ice in his drink tinkled thinly as he swilled it around. He muttered something about being left out on a limb.

"Not you, Toby," she assured him. "Not the best interviewer and link-man in the business. Tonight, free of the burden of a script, you'll rise to heights undreamed of in TV philosophy. Wait till you read tomorrow's reviews."

Ever susceptible to flattery, particularly from a pretty woman, Jakeman remembered his manners sufficiently to offer to pour Tina a drink.

"Okay, kids. On set, please. Bring your drinks, we'll not start rolling for a while yet." This was Gerald Hackett-Bryce, high-flying director of "The Pathologist," who had early cottoned on to the highly intelligent, articulate, and beautiful Dr. Tina May while Johnny Kettle was still alive and had slotted her into a weekly topic magazine programme where she had been an instant success.

Lighting tests over, the two protagonists settled themselves in the set, which was got up to represent the library of some elegant professional woman's town house (and vastly different from the tiny room in 18 Lochiel Street that was cluttered with books on every plane surface, and enjoyed the same designation); Tina on a very feminine-looking chintz-covered sofa with scatter cushions; Jakeman sitting bolt up-right in a leather button-back armchair, which made him look like a well-fed interrogator of the Spanish Inquisition about to order another couple of turns of the rack.

They sat like this in an awkward silence, each with their own thoughts—till the signal to begin. As the title and cred-its rolled up on the monitor, they were "discovered" in an animated, soundless conversation which in fact related to the weather. The credits over, Jakeman "discovered" their audience, briefly switched on and off his frosty, inquisitorial smile, and went into the standard opening spiel:

"Good evening. Tonight, I bring you once more Dr. Tina May, renowned forensic pathologist and sleuth extraordi-nary, in another of her astonishing programmes, where she reveals the truth behind the merely apparent in some of the puzzling cases based on her private files." He paused to let that sink in, allowed himself a pregnant pause, and contin-ued: "In fact, Dr. May is going to devote this entire programme to one particular case, which, I am assured, is one of particular relevance to the times in which we live . . ."

Jakeman, who was a professional to his stubby fingertips and had not the faintest idea what Tina was going to unleash upon him, was already ad-libbing in hope and, though possessing neither bricks nor straw, was building out his part with customary mastery.

He turned to look across at Tina, who was half seated, half reclining on the elegant sofa like some latter-day Madame Récamier. The camera embraced them both.

"Dr. May, without further ado, I ask you to unfold the mystery and see if I—or any of our viewers—can anticipate your findings and solve this case of a crime—a crime which you, yourself, unravelled by the art and science of forensic pathology."

This was the standard opener and introduction for Tina to begin her spiel. The camera closed in on her. She made a pretence of consulting a clipboard that lay on her lap, looked up at the viewer with a serious expression, and began:

"Some few months ago, I was summoned to attend a house in North London where the body of a sixty-year-old retired schoolmaster—a widower—had been discovered by his daily cleaning woman, who, receiving no answer to her knock . . ."

The vision had switched to a stock shot of Tina walking down a quiet suburban street and turning into the gate of a solid-looking Edwardian terrace house. There was a helmeted police officer at the door. He saluted Tina. (This was a slice of the incredible amount of footage that had been shot before the series started, showing Tina in every conceivable cliché situation; costumed in sequence, dressed to suit all weathers, with backgrounds of sun, rain, snow. The entire enterprise had taken over two weeks to film.)

"The body had been discovered by the cleaning woman in the drawing room at the rear of the house, fully dressed and seated in an armchair. The police detectives were in attendance. I was asked to give my opinion as to cause of death . . ."

Vision switched to a shot of Tina with a pair of stock detective types beside her, all in half-length. True to the policy of the series, the presence of the body was only obliquely indicated. After a soundless exchange with one of her companions, Tina leaned forward towards the viewer and reached out a hand as if to touch the unseen victim.

"I formed the opinion that death was attributable to asphyxia, though there were no signs of strangulation. However, I was prepared to stand by my opinion, confident that the post-mortem would show further and more definite evidence . . ."

It was here that Toby Jakeman, true to his role of the Man You Love to Hate, interposed his first objection. This he did in his carefully assumed, blustering, hectoring manner—which the uncharitable among his acquaintances asserted to be only dear Toby playing his ghastly self:

"Now, hold on, wait a minute, Doctor! You have this body sitting in an easy chair. No marks of strangulation, no rope around the neck, nothing. Yet you immediately leap to the conclusion that he's been asphyxiated. Have I got it right— that's what you said, wasn't it?"

Close-up of Tina with a small smile lingering at the corners of her lips. "That is so, Mr. Jakeman. There are other causes of asphyxia than strangulation."

"Well, perhaps you'd care to name a few."

"There's drowning . . ."

"So, his murderer—supposing it's a murder and not suicide—drowns him in the bath, then dresses him and carries him downstairs and puts him in an armchair.

"Likely, isn't it?" With this went the by now famous Jakeman sneer.

Switch to Tina, quite unruffled, still smiling. "Asphyxia may also be caused by the inhalation of certain fumes—as, for instance, in a fire."

"A fire! So—our victim is seated in the armchair, fully dressed, with his house burnt down all round him!"

Close-up of Tina again, expression denoting more sorrow than anger. "Mr. Jakeman, one could be forgiven for thinking that you're trying to be facetious . . ."

In the control room, Simon Elles and Gerald Hackett-Bryce missed not a move, not a nuance of expression recorded on the bank of monitors and loud speakers, where the technicians balanced sound and switched from one camera to another.

"It's hot!" said Elles. "I thought Toby might flounder—that was me forgetting he's the best man in his line of business. And, God, how Tina leads him by the nose—real artistry! This is what this show's all about, man—the content doesn't matter a damn—the manner's everything!"

"Allowing that that pair never get around to liking each other," observed Hackett-Bryce, "this show could outlive 'em all!"

The enthusiasm of producer and director never flagged throughout the one-hour programme, and everyone who was not doing anything particular at the time crowded into any place where there was a monitor functioning from "The Pathologist" set. At the close of it, Simon Elles sat back in his seat and let his imagination run to buying a yacht to grace his villa in Sardinia.

"No need for any editing, Simon, do you reckon?" prompted Hackett-Bryce.

"Not a word," responded the other. "Let it go out just as it is—it'll be a sensation!"

TEN

Derek Arkwright's secretary, who took the message, had relayed Tina May's recommendation to look in on her Monday night programme, and Arkwright, who never missed the show, made special provision to do so; on that special occasion, he and Turner—both bachelors—supped in the Yard canteen that evening and were back in the latter's office in time to see the closing minutes of the previous programme on the big screen TV.

Turner bridged the hiatus by enquiring after his chief's mother and her broken hip, and how was he coping alone at home? Arkwright responded that broken hip-bones are the very devil for the elderly and that he had got himself a temporary housekeeper to fill in. That brought them up to eight o'clock and the opening of "The Pathologist."

The credits over, Jakeman began his opening patter, and presently switched his attention to Tina. Both watching men experienced a lifting of the spirits to see her half-reclining on her sofa, for all the world like a society hostess and totally disassociated in one's mind from the sobriquet of "Corpse Doctor" which the gutter press was forever trying to hang on to her.

There followed her exchange with Jakeman, and her cool manner of putting him down—which greatly amused the two watching detectives.

Her presentation continued . . .

The camera closed in on Tina and she addressed the viewer: "By this time, the police had established several very significant facts about the dead man, whom I will refer to as Mr. D.

"Upon his retirement, he had expressed an intention to buy himself a small beachside villa on one of the Spanish costas, and it was established, by application to Mr. D.'s bank, that there had indeed been sufficient funds on deposit to make the down payment on such a villa, and an adequate pension to service the life insurance which would secure the property outright upon his reaching the age of seventy.

"I say that there *had* been sufficient funds . . ." She paused and looked meaningfully into the camera.

Arkwright shifted uncomfortably in his seat. "I don't know about you, Turner," he said, "but suddenly, this tale of Tina's is taking on a significantly familiar ring!"

Switch to Jakeman, leaning forward incisively: pointing a finger, every inch the Grand Inquisitor. "*What* are you implying, Dr. May?" he demanded.

Zoom in on Tina's impassive countenance. "The day before his death, Mr. D. withdrew every penny in his deposit account, amounting to over five thousand pounds . . .

"In cash!"

Arkwright bounded to his feet. "I knew it!" he cried. "She's concocted that story on the lines of the syndrome!"

"My syndrome!" wailed Turner. "She's pinched my syndrome!"

Innocent of any knowledge of the Turner Syndrome, unaware that the evening's presentation of "The Pathologist" contained any arcane reference to the series of crimes which were currently baffling Scotland Yard, Marcus Struthers, Q.C., had tuned in to the presentation, as he religiously did every Tuesday, in order to enjoy the company—however vicariously—of the one woman he admired above all others. And greatly coveted.

She was there, and all perfection. Dressed like that, looking like that, he could imagine her waiting his return from the courts, or from the House. There would be dry martinis made just the way he liked them; he would take the glass from her hand, sit down beside her and tell her about his day.

He frowned, as that bloated swine Jakeman pitched into her, raising some entirely spurious objection to her dissertation—completely destroying the image that he had conjured up in his imagination. With a quiet curse, he stabbed at the sound button and cut the swine's diatribe to silence. Yes, silence was best. Let him but look at her and fantasize his own dialogue . . .

The vision switched to Tina in a white clinical coat, her dazzling, ash-blond hair tucked under a surgical cap. The setting was presumably a mortuary and she was performing some grisly dissection of the victim in question—the schoolmaster johnny she had been discussing before that bastard Jakeman started leading off again. With her was another figure in white, beyond him one of the detectives who had figured in the opening shot of the reconstruction: he was looking pretty sick.

Her profile was turned towards the camera, and with his eyes he traced the perfection of line that ran from her smooth brow, down the unbelievable straightness of her almost classically Grecian nose, to those sensitive lips that offset the quite determined jawline.

God, what a fool he had been to panic that night in Ravello! But for that absurd encounter, where might their relationship have progressed by now?

And it had all been so futile. That fellow had not seen them together, and if he had—what matter? Times have changed, and one's absurd overidentification with lower-middle-class attitudes was totally out of kilter with contemporary classless morals and mores.

The picture had now returned to the studio set, with Tina and Jakeman hammering away at each other, and she so obviously gaining the upper hand in her argument; laying down the law and marking off debating points on her fingers, while that hulking great bladder of lard could only bluster, expostulate, and squirm.

What a woman! What a consort for a man of ambition! . . .

"Sir Marcus and Lady Struthers," he tried it aloud on his tongue, and then progressed: "The Lord Struthers and Lady Struthers." And then, as a variant to them being announced at some function at the Palace, he dressed her in county tweeds and read out the caption under the picture in a glossy society weekly: "Tina, Lady Struthers presenting prizes at the Mummerset Hunter Trials . . ."

Never letting his eyes lose the screen, he edged his way to the drinks table and poured himself a stiff measure of Scotch. Then, turning out all the lights save one wall sconce, he settled himself down to regale himself in the silent presence of Tina May, who might yet be his one day, if only he could contrive some way back into her good graces, so that they could start again from where he in his folly had so stupidly and unfeelingly severed their extremely promising relationship.

Relationship be damned! Let's not be mealy-mouthed, Struthers! We were on our way to bed together when you showed the white feather and chickened out on her!

He had an impulse to throw his half-emptied glass against the far wall—but his hand was stayed by a full-face close-up of the woman who was his obsession.

The living room of Farrell's cottage was barely furnished: a gate-legged table bearing the remains of his supper, a couple of chairs, a bookcase crammed with well-scuffed paperbacks, an easy chair, and a small table upon which stood a tiny black-and-white TV set that surely rated as a museum piece.

The falconer was slumped in the easy chair, a can of lager in his left hand, his right bearing the hawking glove. Perched upon his fist was the eyas goshawk named Baby: she was tearing voraciously at a piece of meat which her master was holding between his gloved thumb and forefinger. Farrell's whole attention was devoted to the flickering screen before him, where the eye of faith could dimly discern the content of the "Pathologist" programme.

Jakeman was leading forth—pontificating in his plummy, fat man's voice: "If I may stem your *most* interesting dissertation, Doctor, and recapitulate . . . You tell me that your post-mortem examination confirmed your earlier view—that the victim died from asphyxia. There were, you said, unmistakable indications . . ."

Tina nodded. "In addition to the small haemorrhages on the face which first led me to that conclusion, I found cyanotic congestion of the organs, notably the lungs and . . ."

"I see, I see." Part of Jakeman's technique of denigration was to cut short any move on Tina's part to introduce medical terminology; implying that she was trying to pull the wool over the eyes of honest laymen. "In addition to that, you also claim to have found traces of our old friend the barbiturate in the stomach. If I may say so, there always seems an awful lot of barbiturate around in your cases, Doctor."

Tina shrugged. "Barbiturates, in the form of sleeping capsules, are easily available on prescription, Mr. Jakeman, and are statistically the most common agents of suicide in the developed world."

Jakeman brushed that aside. "So what do we have? Your Mr. D., who presumably has abandoned the idea of buying a retirement villa in Spain and has drawn out his savings in cash (but more of that later), now decides to end it all, in the furtherance of which he swallows—how many sleeping capsules?"

"A fatal dose—and more. I wouldn't wish to divulge any gratuitous information to would-be suicides, Mr. Jakeman."

"Quite, quite—very commendable of you." Jakeman let slip the edge of a sneer for good value. "So—having ingested a fatal dose of barbiturate, Mr. D. then proceeds to hasten the process by giving himself asphyxia. You have not as yet particularised how he managed to contrive this feat—

though we have already eliminated drowning in the bath and the inhalation of toxic fumes. What else remains, Doctor?"

"The body was found with a plastic bag entirely covering the head. This led to death through asphyxia in a very short space of time."

Collapse of stout party. Jakeman stared at the woman before him, and the camera zoomed in close to register his expression of indignation and affront.

"But you said nothing about any plastic bag when the issue of asphyxia first arose!"

Tina smiled: it was a gentle, conciliatory smile. "You didn't ask me, Mr. Jakeman. You were much too busy trying to be facetious."

To give him his professional due, Jakeman made a good, quick recovery from his setback. He squirmed in his seat and glowered for a while—then returned to the attack with an oblique thrust to the flank, so to speak: "And having contrived this extraordinarily complicated suicide, how did Mr. D. then dispose of the very large amount of cash which, as you have told me, has never been found?"

Tina May paused a few moments before replying: "He had already given it to his executioner—*as payment in advance!*"

The eyas goshawk bated off Farrell's fist with a squawk of alarm. Farrell recovered the winged predator and soothed her by gently stroking her speckled breast.

The master of absorbing a set-back, Toby Jakeman, eschewing aggressiveness for the time being, contented himself by getting as much hard information as he could. So far, he had handled his end of the encounter with Tina May calling all the shots and—it might be said unfairly—holding back one vital fact. What he needed now was to know the rest of the unwritten script.

"You speak of Mr. D.'s executioner, Doctor. Can you clarify that? Why did he need an executioner—why pay someone to kill him when he had an attractive retirement in the sun to look forward to? Did you, perhaps, in your post-mortem examination discover that he was suffering from a painful and terminal illness—and it just so happens that you didn't get around to mentioning it?"

Tina shook her head. "Physically, Mr. D. was as fit and robust as any man of sixty who has looked after his health and is untouched by disease. Unfortunately, a post-mortem can't reveal the subject's mental state at the time of death."

"Are you suggesting—say—depression, Doctor?"

Tina nodded. "They had no children, no relations, and few friends, but he and his wife talked of nothing but their dream home in the sun, and counted the months to his early retirement."

"But she died . . ."

"Then I think he couldn't face up to it alone. So he made plans to follow her."

"But why the executioner?"

Tina looked down at her folded hands, and her voice took on a profound gravity. "Like a lot of would-be suicides, he found that it's the loneliest task in the world, and couldn't go through with it without some moral support and practical help. In the end, he found someone who was willing to play God: to supervise the taking of the capsules and then, when unconsciousness supervened, to put a plastic bag over the victim's head and bring him to a quick end."

Jakeman looked doubtful. "But how do you know he was unconscious when the bag was put over his head? He could have done it himself before the capsules took effect."

Tina May shook her head. "He was unconscious. The bag was fitted neatly over the head and neck and quite undisturbed. Conscious and in his death throes, the victim would have made a frantic attempt to tear off the bag. There was no sign of any such attempt."

"But—the money?"

"Mr. D. had no use for it. He gave it to his executioner, who had explained that his great movement of positive euthanasia would one day spread its blessings worldwide, but before that great day dawned there would have to be much lobbying—maybe suborning—of politicians, the exercising of influence in the highest places—and money, money, money to bring it about. That's how I imagine the executioner rationalised his—activity. But I don't really know. Here, I'm in the field of wildest speculation. But he was almost certainly sincere."

There followed a speculative and philosophical argument which expanded to fill the remaining few minutes of the one hour programme. The two protagonists were still at it—and no pretences of idle chatter about the weather—when the credits unrolled over their soundless discourse.

At the end of it, Farrell got up, stretched himself; then, transferring the eyas to the padded backrest of the easy chair, tied the end of her leash to the arm and went to fetch himself another can of lager.

"That's it! She's got it! Tina's hit the nail right on the head!"

Both Arkwright and Turner were on their feet and ad-libbing:

"The missing money element fits everywhere!"

"And the attempts in every case to make it look like suicide . . ."

"Ah—except for Mrs. Pouter, sir—don't forget the all-in wrestler tip!"

Arkwright waved the objection aside. "That could have been an aberration," he countered. "The executioner—the all-in wrestler type—lost his head when Mrs. Pouter chickened out at the last moment and had to finish her off slovenly."

"Sir—what now?"

"Now, Turner, we build on Tina's hypothesis. We assume that this thing is as potentially big as she imagined it might be when she was—as she put it—in the field of wildest speculation, with politicians and big shots being lobbied and bribed all over the place. We take it that what we've seen so far is only the tip of the iceberg!" He sat down at his desk and, stabbing a recorder button, extemporised into a micro-phone: "I want half a page on every murder and suicide, solved or unsolved, in the Home Counties during the last six months, delivered on my desk before midnight, together with any report—however far-fetched and fanciful—of extortion by threat or promise.

"Tomorrow, I want reports in from every branch of every bank in the same area of any large and unusual withdrawals of cash by private customers." He pressed another button which automatically relayed the taped message to the Control Room in the basement. He then grinned fiercely up at his assistant.

"As for you and me, Turner," he said, "we're going to pay a visit and follow up a clue which we have somewhat neglected."

Snatching up their hats and coats, they left.

They went to the address near Tooting Bec Common: a cul-de-sac of small 1930s semi-detached houses in the vaguely Tudor style, with mature gardens and trees. It spoke of stolid respectability at the lower end of the middle social scale. A row of street lamps shone thinly through the Japanese flowering cherry trees that also lined the sidewalk. They went up to the front door of the house named La Sirène and Turner rang the bell. Neither that nor a second ring brought any response.

"We'll sweat it out in the car," said Arkwright.

They remained parked two doors up from La Sirène. At that hour of the night there was not much activity in Cherry Tree Close, nor would there likely be till pub-closing time. There were a few lights in the windows around them, but most folks in that area reserved the front rooms for "best" and spent most of their time in the sitting room overlooking the garden to the rear, which was almost invariably the TV room.

"Dr. May, she's a deep one, sir," observed Turner.

"She has her methods," declared Arkwright. "It was certainly a good way of selling her theory—putting it out in her programme so that only a very limited number of people at the Yard would get the message."

"And the executioner, sir," prompted Turner.

"Yes—that's a thought," said Arkwright. "Not that the warning's going to do him any good: he's left too broad a trail, too many unravelled ends, to be able to close down his activities and fade away into obscurity."

"I was thinking of Dr. May's safety, sir."

"She'll be all right. We'll put a guard on her till the executioner's been rounded up. That should be tonight, or some time tomorrow." He reached out for the "transmit" button of the radio. "I'll fix a surveillance on her from now till . . ."

Turner stayed his hand. "Someone's coming, sir."

There was the sound of footfalls entering the close to their rear.

Instinctively, Turner sank lower in the driver's seat. Glancing sidelong at his chief, he saw the other's profile etched against the loom of the street lamp immediately behind them; Arkwright was gazing stonily ahead.

Nearer came the footfalls. Presently, a long shadow cast ahead of the newcomer by the street lamp was displayed along the pavement before the watching detectives: the elongated shadow of a man in an overcoat and a close-fitting hat that might have been a beret; Turner had the immediate impression that he was a soldier.

When the figure came abreast and moved ahead, it was altogether shorter, stockier, more heavily built than the elongated shadow had suggested.

The two detectives watched the newcomer slow down, pause, and enter the gate of La Sirène.

"Come on!" muttered Arkwright. "Let's get it over with!"

Together they slipped out of the car and, without slamming the doors behind them, moved quickly and silently upon their quarry, whom they overtook half-way down the path to the front door of the house.

Arkwright reached out a hand and touched the other's

shoulder, just as an alarmed, wide-eyed stare was turned upon him.

" 'Evening, Miss Slyte," he said to the retired infant school headmistress. "Do you know, I've only just figured out what kind of guidance your friend the late Miss Waterhouse was seeking from her mother who had passed over. Would you like to ask us in and talk about it?"

The first fear having passed, the mannish-looking female in slacks, with the close-cropped grey hair tucked under a beret, seemed to gain a certain dignity. "Come in, Mr. Arkwright," she said, "and let's talk by all means. I always said to myself that if you found me out I would deny nothing.

"What I've done, I've done with my eyes wide open, knowing the quality of my acts. And I've no regrets.

"This way," she added, opening the front door. "And mind the step—the light isn't working in the hallway."

Arkwright was back again in his office by eleven, and the reports were already piling up on his desk. Turner had opted to come with him, though he had been on duty since dawn.

They had brought Miss Slyte back with them. The ex-headmistress was now in the charge of the duty WPO and comfortably bedded down in a cell that scarcely deserved to be graced by such a depreciatory honorific. Her pug dog was in care. Miss Slyte was to be charged in the morning.

Arkwright's first thought was to be put through to the senior officer of the two patrol cars which were stationed at Lochiel Street:

". . . All well?"

"Her light went out half an hour ago, sir. All quiet."

"Keep your heads down. I don't want Dr. May to be worried. If she goes out in the morning, have her discreetly tailed by your two plainclothesmen. That's all."

"Message understood, sir. Roger and out."

Arkwright made a neat pile of the half-page reports he had ordered, took a sip of his coffee, and addressed himself to the task of gutting them.

"Unless you want any help with that, sir," said Turner, "I'll dictate my notes on Miss Slyte's statement and have it typed up for her to sign in the morning. Unless she's changed her tune by then, that is."

Arkwright shook his head. "She won't budge an inch from the truth," he said, "and that's what she gave us tonight. Our only concern now is that she can't possibly be the muscle man who broke Mrs. Pouter's neck, which means that there's at least one other party concerned in the syndrome." He tapped the sheaf of papers before him. "Our man might turn up somewhere in here."

Alone, Arkwright began to wade through the reports, which told of suicide, murder, and extortion. On the first going-through, with a perfunctory glance at each, he had them divided into three piles. On the eeny-meeny-miny-mo principle, he first plumped for the one comprising extortion by threat or promise. They largely concerned attempts by small-time suburban villains to set up protection rackets; cases of petty blackmail directed against erring husbands, back-street jewellers who received bits and pieces of stolen property, and suchlike. None of these seemed to have any bearing on the Turner syndrome—until he came to a very businesslike report on an interview with a Mrs. Teresa Vallence of Finchley, conducted by a WPC Daisy Burton, who—from the manner in which she had handled the incident—seemed to be a young woman with a head on her shoulders.

The report had Arkwright sending down a recorded message to the Control Room: "Top priority. Tomorrow morning at a civilised hour—say, about ten o'clock—call upon Mrs. Teresa Vallence at her home at 13 Parkway Close, Finchley. Tactfully persuade Mrs. Vallence back to the Yard, where DCI Arkwright has news of the man she knows as Norman, which will be of interest to her."

The remainder of the reports—including the extras that came in before the midnight deadline—took him till nearly three o'clock to winnow through. And nothing in them suggested a connection with the syndrome—there was only

Daisy Burton's curiously evocative account of her interview with Mrs. Vallence.

His task done, Arkwright slumped down in his comfortable leather armchair and was asleep before he had time to enjoy the wonder of closing his eyes and letting everything go.

Mrs. Vallence was more than delighted to accept the handsome young police officer's suggestion that she accompany him back to Scotland Yard, but insisted on a complete change of costume for the occasion. This comprised a smart spring coat worn over a tweed skirt, blouse with a tie neck, and a bolero. As always, she wore hat and gloves. It was nearly half-past eleven when the patrol car drew in by the main entrance to the Yard and Mrs. Vallence was handed over to a messenger who guided her up to Arkwright's office.

He rose upon her entry, and she had a clear impression of a shy man. Perhaps it was the heavy glasses which gave him the look of a scholar and a recluse. The voice that invited her to sit down was gentle, and with overtones of the West Country burr. He introduced the man with him: a shortish, quirky-looking individual with dark-circled eyes—as Detective Sergeant Turner. He looked tired, poor man.

"Mrs. Vallence," said Arkwright, "have you heard anything further from Norman?"

She hastened to assure him that she had not. "But he said he'd ring me in a week's time, you see? And that will be the day after tomorrow," she added.

"Quite. Now—can you perhaps expand upon the appearance of this man that you gave to the woman police constable at Meresham Road? You say here that he's strongly built, tough-looking, very masculine. Can you particularise on that, please? Colour of hair and eyes? Complexion? Any visible scars? And do you think you could identify him from a photograph?"

Yes, he had sandy hair, pale blue eyes. A rather sallow complexion with that craggy face. No scars that she noticed

—and, yes, she would know him from a photograph quite easily.

"Then I'd like you to go along with Detective Sergeant Turner, who'll show you some pictures," said Arkwright, rising.

Ushered out by Turner, Mrs. Vallence paused—as Arkwright posed a final question: "Ma'am, just one point. After he claimed to have left the Army, did Norman give you any hint as to the civilian occupation he took up?"

"No, he didn't, but I would have put him down as doing something very *physical.* Like a professional boxer, or a weight lifter. You know what I mean? He was very *strong* to look at."

Armstrong and Turner exchanged glances.

Turner's transcripted edition of the verbal statement that Miss Slyte had given them the night before, along with coffee and biscuits in the neat front room of her little house in Cherry Tree Close, had occupied only a small part of that eminent detective's efforts in the early hours. It was brief, to the point, and Arkwright read it with interest and approval:

Form H.M.S.O. 693 (B) Metropolitan Police	

The Written Statement of Miss Nancy Jane Slyte, of La Sirene, Cherry Tree Close, Tooting, London. Given on today's date.
 	
    This statement is given by me of my own free will, having been cautioned as to my rights by Detective Sergeant Turner.
    I was approached to join a small and select society set up to practise positive euthanasia among the
	/Who took the Statement

suffering and needy. Since I have always had strong convictions in this line (my own father died after a painful and protracted illness and many was the time that he begged me to give him more of the pills and put him out of his misery), I needed little persuasion, feeling that this was my opportunity to do something meaningful with the rest of my life.

/To be checked with Registrar

I have no intention of involving the person who inducted me into the society. Though willing to pay for my transgression against what I consider to be a bad law, I utterly refuse to implicate the other party.

/Believed to be a male person

I met Miss Clarice Waterhouse at Graveley Road Spiritualist Church. She told me she was seeking guidance from her late mother as to whether she should make an end of herself. Miss Waterhouse suffered from an advanced cancer of the throat and spoke only with difficulty.

/Founded 1924 and of good Repute

In short, I assisted her to leave. After she had taken the capsules in the bath, I waited till she was unconscious, then, taking her by the ankles, gently slid her face under water. She passed away quickly and peacefully, and I had no regrets, then or after.

/This account conforms with Dr May's post mortem report

Yes, I had persuaded Miss Waterhouse to donate a large sum

/Ms Slyte admitted this

of money for the furtherance of the society, but I refuse to divulge how I disposed of it.
(Signed)

much only with reluctance

Turner took Mrs. Vallence in a lift to the basement, and ushered her into a small, luxuriously appointed movie auditorium where the two of them took comfortable seats in the centre of the middle row.

"The idea's quite simple, Mrs. Vallence," explained the detective. "The basic appearance that you gave to Mr. Arkwright has already been passed down here. In a few moments, you'll see mug shots—that's to say photos in full face and profile—of men in our records who most nearly fit that description. All you have to do is to say out loud if you don't see the right man, and particularise as to why, such as—the hair line's too high, the nose too long, the eyes not wide enough apart. In very swift succession these fine adjustments of appearance will be taken into account. You'll see the faces change up there on the screen to conform with your slightest correction. In no time at all, Mrs. Vallence, if we have a photographic record of Norman—you'll be looking at him. Any questions?"

She shook her head.

"Lights!" said Turner. "Let's go!"

The first face appeared, head on and in profile, side by side.

"Too old," whispered the woman, nudging Turner.

"Louder, Mrs. Vallence," said the latter, "as if you're talking to the guy up there on the screen."

"Too old!" repeated Mrs. Vallence. "The eyes should be a paler blue, and the lips are too full."

Such is the miracle of electronic selection that within three seconds, another face appeared that bore the amended characteristics which the woman had ordered.

"No," said Mrs. Vallence. Another and similar face took its place.

"No."

Another . . .

"No."

Another, another, another and another—all dismissed and immediately replaced upon her declaration.

"He was fuller round here," said Mrs. Vallence, gesturing with her hands. "Round the—do you call them—jowls?"

Another face—bejowled—came up on the screen.

"That's more like him," she exclaimed.

"Run that set of characteristics right through," ordered Turner.

"No—no—no—no—no—no," cried Mrs. Vallence in quick time, and just as quickly another mug shot came up.

Till . . .

"That's him! That's Norman—I'd know him anywhere!"

"Well done, Mrs. Vallence," said Turner, much relieved.

"The name's Wain, sir," said Turner. "Edward Thomas Wain, aged forty-seven, born Newcastle-on-Tyne. Served as a physical-training instructor in the Royal Marines. Discharged for theft with violence. Served three terms for robbery with violence and another for malicious wounding. Latterly turned to—would you believe it?—doing a strong-man act at workingmen's clubs. You know the kind of thing: tearing up telephone directories and picking up the two fattest men in the audience, two-handed."

"That accounts for the all-in wrestling angle," said Arkwright.

"Yes, and he latterly turned to busking to theatre queues," continued Turner, "and became quite a well-known character around theatreland, even appeared in the "In Town" spot on TV with his act. We shouldn't have much difficulty in picking him up, now that we've got his name and face."

Arkwright looked thoughtful. "One jarring note," he said. "Does Wain—Norman—strike you as the sort of character who'd persuade a sincere person like Miss Slyte to join his society?"

"She wouldn't have taken much persuading," responded the other. "And, anyhow, we know from Mrs. Vallence that he's got one hell of a way with the ladies."

"We'll see," said Arkwright. "Put out a general call. Circulate his mug shot to all stations. Organise a 'Have you seen this Man?' item on tonight's TV. Send a squad round the theatre queues and bring in anyone who claims a passing acquaintance with him, like taking him for a drink. I want him in before midnight."

In the event, Arkwright's time of aspiration was greatly advanced by a call from the Baker Street police station. The previous day, they had had the sort of complaint that inevitably gets filed away and forgotten. A certain Mrs. Settle, occupation—cleaner, who had worked for a disabled spinster lady in York Terrace, Regent's Park, claimed that her mistress's part-time chauffeur had got her the sack as daily woman so that he could, in Mrs. Settle's phrase: "Feather his nest" and she wouldn't be surprised if "this Norman feller didn't do Miss Tewson in, 'cos he looked the sort who'd strangle his own mother for the week's rent."

All cars were homed in on York Terrace.

"Let's go, Turner!" cried Arkwright.

The phone rang as he was snatching up his coat; Turner answered it.

"It's Dr. May, sir," he said.

"I'll take it," said Arkwright.

"Derek . . ."

"Tina, you've won the game. You were right. It's a positive euthanasia conspiracy. We've got one party and we're just moving in to grab the other one."

"But—who *are* these people, Derek?"

"You'd scarcely believe it—a retired infant school headmistress and a guy who tore up telephone directories for a living. It's a strange world we live in. I must go. See you later, Tina."

" 'Bye, Derek."

It was with a curious lightness of heart that Tina May made herself a cup of coffee and reflected that a weight had been lifted from her conscience. Yes, she had *used* Jamie Farrell as a kind of guinea pig to assemble her hypothesis, but no harm had come of it, and he surely would have telephoned in high dudgeon if he had recognised anything of himself and his own philosophy in her peroration; but, then, they always say that people never see any resemblance to themselves in either fact or fiction—even when the resemblance is hilariously obvious to everyone else.

She would make it up with Jamie, for he wasn't a bad sort —only a bit bloody-minded, and she had arguably overreacted about the killing of the hare.

She would get in touch with him as soon as possible and take him out for a drink. Yes, that would be the best way to mend her fences.

ELEVEN

Edward Thomas Wain, also known as Norman, had good cause to be quite pleased with himself that morning as he went to fetch the Daimler from the mews garage. All was going well: in big things as in small, Miss Tewson was practically eating out of his hands. As regards small, he had prevailed upon her that their daily car outings be reduced to twice weekly on the score of economy: it had been so long since she had had use of the Daimler, and so much had happened in the world between times, that the news of the current price of gasoline had come as a traumatic shock, and she had readily agreed to a curtailment of her trips out. This suited Norman's plans very well, for the less he was seen abroad with his intended victim the better, and even then he had taken to wearing dark glasses. For the same reason, he always dissuaded her from stopping off anywhere in his company. Till he was ready to make his move, the best thing was for both of them to be shut up together at her place, all nice and cosy—and unseen.

He opened the garage doors and ran his hand over the gleaming bonnet of the limousine. This would fetch a penny or two as well; not many veterans in this tip-top condition. As for the contents of the apartment—well, during the spell he'd spent as porter in that West End antique dealer's, he'd learned a few things about tip-top furniture and pictures. No need to arouse anyone's suspicions at the bank by getting the old lady to draw out unusually large amounts—best to hire a self-drive van and take away a fortune in portable goods, stash the stuff in a lock-up garage and dribble it on to the market, piece by piece. Very smart!

It only remained to decide upon the manner of her going, and it didn't really matter which way. With a bit more groundwork, he could persuade her that it simply wasn't worth while going on (she had already practically figured that out for herself). Maybe if he told her he was leaving her —yes!—that might push her over the edge. Anyhow, in the last resort, he could top her like he'd topped Alice Pouter— except that a nice tidy suicide looked better.

Still happily cogitating, he climbed into the driving seat. The magnificent engine murmured discreetly into life, and a few minutes later he was turning into York Terrace, where there seemed to be an unusually large accumulation of cars . . .

Miss Tewson, dressed all in black—a distinctive figure— was waiting for him at the top of the steps leading to the front door. She was not alone.

What he saw next—when he had taken a second look at the quality of the assembled cars, not to mention the appearance of the men who were grouped on the step with Miss Tewson —brought his foot down on the accelerator, impelling the cruising Daimler into a tyre-screeching explosion of speed. He traversed across half of the noble façade of York Terrace and was out of York Gate and tearing into the mid-morning traffic of Marylebone Road just as the police sirens reached out their two-toned threat behind him.

Ahead lay Baker Street, and the traffic lights were against him. Three red double-decker London buses, a couple of taxi cabs, and a pantechnicon were halted there in line. In his rear-view mirror, he could see the lead police car cutting out to overtake the vehicles that barred its path; wrenching at the wheel, the man called Norman swerved to do likewise. He sliced past the waiting line and rocketed out across busy Baker Street—and slammed into the side of a delivery van, braking savagely as he went. The other vehicle's rear tyres blew out and it settled down on its hunkers with the long bonnet of the Daimler half into the piles of crates and boxes that comprised its interior.

Norman, dazed, lifted his head from the steering wheel, with which his brow had made stunning contact, to hear the police sirens closing all about him. Wrenching open the driver's door, he staggered out into the street, ducked under the arm of a perfectly well-intentioned pedestrian who had come forward to help him, and lighted across the road towards the entrance of the Underground station. Half-a-dozen of the police, seeing what he was at, abandoned their vehicles and raced in pursuit.

Down the steps, leaping three at a time, elbowing aside all who got in his way: a juggernaut on the run down a crowded passageway, tumbling people left and right. Out into the booking hall and across to the barrier and the head of the escalators. He burst his way through the barrier, where a black face bawled something incomprehensible at him—and then he was plunging down the moving escalator, with the nearest, youngest, and most athletic of his pursuers not ten yards behind and yelling after him to stop.

A gusting of warm air from out of a nearby tunnel suggested the nearness of a train and he dived towards it—to emerge onto a crowded platform and not a train in sight.

"Stop where you are—you're cornered now!" The declaration was backed up by the presence of no fewer than four blue-clad figures moving up behind him.

Only one line of escape . . .

They shouted warnings to him as, stooping, he vaulted lightly down into the pit that ran between the two outer rails, and from out of which arose the supports for the middle, live rail. A ready hand reached swiftly down to grab him by the shoulder, and would have done so—but was prudently withdrawn before contact.

Police and horrified travellers stood and watched as the fugitive plunged forward into the train tunnel, his coat tails flirting within inches of instant death from the centre rail. Without a backward glance, he went under the low archway, into the darkness, and was out of sight.

A police sergeant said: "He's heading for Great Portland

Street and it's only a short hop. Radio for a reception committee to be waiting for him on the platform—if he makes it.

"And have 'em switch off the power in this section—pronto!"

The grumbling giant announced his coming from out of the bowels of the earth, and the blood chilled. Louder and louder, closer and closer he came, and the ground shook. Instinctively, they all backed away from the edge of the platform, pressing themselves against the tiled wall of the vault, watching the maw of the tunnel with unwinking eyes.

Above the bursting sound of the incoming train, there were some who heard a last, despairing scream.

There were more screams all round when the train exploded into view, displaying on its front the rags of what had been a man; bearing its burden into Baker Street station and gliding to a gentle halt as the power was switched off—too late—along that entire section of the Inner Circle line.

An empty coffee cup and a half-eaten ham sandwich that represented the remains of Arkwright's lunch still lay on his desk when they ushered in Miss Slyte and more or less pushed her into the chair before the scowling man in the heavy library glasses.

"Miss Slyte," he said, "last night, I was inclined to take you at your face value, accept your sincerity and treat you as a special case. The way I saw it, given the right kind of judge and jury, you were a cinch for manslaughter and a suspended sentence.

"The happenings of this morning, however, have greatly altered my views. For my money, you deserve the book to be thrown at you—and you may be sure that I shall do anything in my power to bring about that well-deserved state of affairs."

The woman, who had been regarding him with puzzlement admixed with alarm, shook her head and stammered a response to his outburst:

"Mr. Arkwright, I—I don't know what to say. I've made my

position clear. Certainly, I haven't implicated my associate, but for my part I've been frank. And nothing's changed since last night."

Arkwright leaned forward and replied with a savagery that Turner—who was standing by—had never seen displayed by his chief.

"It's well said, Miss Slyte, that you know a girl by the company she keeps. Well, we have made the acquaintance— briefly, alas—of your accomplice, and the encounter has opened up a whole new field of speculation as to what lies behind that sweet-little-old-lady image you present to the world. Am I being rude? I hope so—and I can assure you that my rudeness is entirely intentional!"

"Mr. Arkwright—what are you trying to tell me?" she asked, and behind the sudden anxiety there was a discernible fortitude of the sort that rises in adversity: the small chin came up, the eyes flashed; Taylor saw her for the first time in the role of headmistress.

Arkwright answered evenly enough: "What shall I tell you that you don't know already, Miss Slyte? That your accomplice is—I should say *was*, for he was killed whilst trying to escape this morning . . ."

"Oh no!" she breathed.

". . . That your accomplice was an old lag with a string of convictions for violent crime, that he certainly killed one of your—I quote you from your statement—'suffering and needy clients,' and in a particularly crude and brutal manner. And that's the only victim we've unearthed so far, though we know of two others he had lined up for slaughter."

She shook her head wildly.

"No—this can't be true!" she cried. "He's not like that. Not he! The man I know is a gentle person, a man of intelligence and understanding, though perhaps lacking warmth in human relationships. It was he who inducted me into the society, explained our objects: how—by the exerting of influence to change the law as regards euthanasia—we would make a new world where unnecessary human suffering was banished. After our one and only meeting was over, we prayed together. At least, I prayed, and he knelt with his head bowed, but took no other part for, as he explained, he was a conscientious agnostic. Oh no, Mr. Arkwright, you are so wrong about him!"

Arkwright then gave tongue to a concept which had been hardening in his mind since the woman had begun her rebuttal: "Miss Slyte," he said quietly, "I don't think we're talking about the same man!"

She glanced up at him sharply; she had been looking down at her hands.

"There were—*others?*" she asked.

"One other, certainly," said Arkwright. He leaned forward, hands and elbows on the desk, gazing at her earnestly. "Miss Slyte," he said, "for the sake of everything you hold dear, you've got to come clean with me. This society of yours has got to be taken apart and submitted to scrutiny, so that we know—and so that *you* know—how many more slaughterers are sailing under your flag."

"What—what can I say?" she asked, bemused.

"Start by telling me about this man who inducted you. Tell me his name, and what means you have of getting in touch with him."

"I've no means of getting in touch with him," she said. "The money contributed by Miss Waterhouse—God rest her soul—I sent, as instructed, to an accommodation address for him to pick up. He was quite frank about that: for reasons of security we must know as little about each other as possible. Which was why we used codes to identify each other, instead of our names. I was 'Mermaid'—La Sirène, you know."

"And he?"

"He called himself—'Birdman.' "

"Turner, you'd better put a guard back on Tina May," said Arkwright. "Give her a ring now and tell her that the gang's bigger than we thought and they're not all rounded up. Do it now—and I'll have a word with her when you've finished."

Putting on earphones, he played through the tape of the conversation—interrogation—that had taken place between him and Miss Slyte a few minutes before. Turner was juggling with the phone; presently he put it down and frowned with annoyance.

"What's the problem?" asked Arkwright, putting aside the earphones.

"I got her answering machine," said Turner, dialling again. "She says in an emergency to call her on Wishford 223—wherever that is."

Arkwright watched him with a certain detached interest; presently Turner sucked his teeth and put the phone down.

"No one's answering," he said.

"Check out the number with Central Registry," said Arkwright.

This Turner did, and the information that is not readily available to the general public—the identity and address of a subscriber obtained from his number—was back within half a minute.

"Well?" prompted Arkwright. "What goes—why are you sitting there looking like you've been hit over the head with a sandbag?"

"The address is Peasbrook Cottage, Wishford, Essex," said Turner. "The subscriber's name is J. Farrell, and he also gives his occupation in the phone book . . ."

"And that is? . . ."

"Falconer!"

"Birdman!"

It was almost like summer, thought Tina. The farther east, the more trees were in full leaf, and the village gardens overspilled with rhododendrons, azaleas, magnolias, and swallows dipped over the low thatched eaves. She came presently to a village green, with a church whose tower must have borne a burning brand for Agincourt and a pub that was old when Drake was a boy. She was in no hurry, for she was not due at Jamie's place till lunchtime, so she stopped off and had half a pint of bitter which she drank at an outside table, enjoying the unseasonably hot sun.

Thank heaven, she thought, that it was all right with Jamie. He had responded to her call with his customary lack of animation, but at least there had been not the slightest sign of resentment; no problem there. And he had had the grace to invite her to lunch out: *out,* mark you—he was not going to submit her to his no doubt typical bachelor cuisine!

She was humming gaily as she got back into the little Mini that the garage had supplied. Her lightheartedness she attributed to the singular success of her TV gambit, through which Derek Arkwright had been able to clear up the Turner syndrome. How very gratifying to be right! She caught her reflexion in the rear-view mirror and put her tongue out at what she saw: easy on the hubris, May—remember that overweening pride goes before a fall!

As she drew nearer Wishford, the rural tranquillity gave way to the raped landscape of ticky-tacky land, and she got stuck behind an enormous gasoline truck on a winding, two-way road. For mile after mile, she soldiered on behind the juggernaut, building up a pressure of exasperation which almost led her to attempt to overtake—and at considerable hazard—on the next short length of straight road that they came upon. Happily, she was spared this indiscretion when the tanker signalled and turned off into a wayside filling station, at the exit of which there stood a little old woman with a large suitcase parked at her heels. She gave Tina a frantic signal for a hitch, and Tina slowed down and stopped beside her.

"Going far?"

"No, dearie—just a mile or two down the road."

"Jump in. Give me your case—it can go on the back seat." The Mini set off again.

"It's a travellers' camp," said the old woman. "You'll see the caravans through the trees." (She pronounced the word as "cara-waans.")

Trust me to pick up a gipsy, thought Tina, who, for all her

liberal education and outlook, had the standard received middle-class belief that all gipsies are both thieves and verminous. She edged away from her companion as far as she could go.

"Going to call on a friend?" asked her passenger.

Amused, Tina acknowledged that she was.

"He's no good," was the surprising announcement.

Tina nearly laughed aloud, but settled for humouring the poor creature. "Possibly not," she said, "but it's really unimportant, because he won't be given the opportunity to be no good to me."

"You'd do best to turn back," said the other.

"I have come rather a long way," countered Tina. "And I *am* promised a meal."

The old woman fell silent—to Tina's relief. To her greater relief, there presently came in sight a cluster of gipsy caravans in a paddock set just off the road, behind a screen of poplar trees. She slowed down the Mini. "Here we are," she said brightly.

The old woman climbed awkwardly out of the little car, and Tina handed her case after her. Their eyes met, and the other's were as black as boot buttons and redolent of ancient sin.

"Best for you to turn back, lady," she said. "There's Death all round you. I see him plain." She turned and was gone, scurrying through last year's long, dead grass.

Tina drove on. "Well, I could have done without the gipsy's warning," she said aloud. "That certainly puts a damper on the proceedings."

She switched on the car radio, but succeeded in getting only the crackle of static and what sounded like electrical disturbance of the thunderstorm kind.

Ahead, to the east, the sky had darkened and was closing down towards her, further overshadowing what had been her holiday mood.

About ten miles from the turn-off to Wishford, the road passed through a forestry area of Norwegian pines in sundry stages of growth from Christmas tree size to towering giants: interminable acres of greenery scored through with fire breaks every half mile or so. It had begun to rain and the windscreen wipers were swim-swamming, the small tyres hissing on the streaming road. Tina's mood was similarly dampened.

Half-way through the forest, she noticed a Land-Rover halted by the end of a fire break and pointing towards the road; she paid no attention as she swept past it, but noticed the vehicle move out after she had gone by and take up station a couple of hundred yards behind her.

"Brought for the Blooding . . ."
The phrase struck the right note in his mind.

He turned to regard the eyas, whose yellow-irised malevolence was turned upon him from her ring perch in the back of the Land-Rover. She was in a nervous state: the plumage clung as closely to her as a sheath dress on a cheap whore, and she threatened to bate, spreading her wings in preparation when the vehicle went over a bump in the road. Once she took off completely and was brought up short at the end of her leash; a pitiful hopping around on the jouncing floor, and she was happy to leap back on to her perch.

"Stay where you are," he said aloud. "You'll be all the better there to see the blooding!" And he resumed his concentration upon the road up ahead.

Some distance from where he had turned out of the forest, the road inclined gradually upwards for two or three miles, while the ground on each side fell away to form an embankment. He waited till this configuration was markedly formed —when there was a drop of about twenty feet or so—then accelerated sharply, closing the gap between the Land-Rover and the Mini ahead.

There was not another vehicle in sight on that wet Wednesday midday in wildest Essex. The driver of the Mini was certainly paying no attention to the nondescript, mud-smeared farmer's vehicle that made as if to overtake. From the corner of his eye (and he was wearing concealing dark shades, as well as a stocking cap pulled well down over his ears), he could see her gazing stonily at the road ahead.

Waiting till his sturdy front wheels were in line with the driver's door of the little saloon car, he wrenched brutally at the steering and sent the massively weighted chassis of the Land-Rover ploughing into the side of the Mini. There was a crash of breaking glass, and the rear window on the near side of the Land-Rover fell into the body in two parts, one of which narrowly missed slicing the eyas goshawk in half; she squawked and bated wildly, distracting her master's concentration. Cursing to find that he was having the greatest difficulty in holding his vehicle on the wet road, he slowed down and allowed the Mini to draw ahead again.

The damage: a slightly crumpled near-side wing on the Land-Rover, a hideous deep dent in the Mini's side, and broken windows in both.

Such was the first figure in that Dance of Death.

Shocked out of a slightly depressed reverie by the unheralded assault, Tina was instantly brought to the necessity of keeping the Mini on the road and herself alive. This she did by the exercising of considerable skill and the blessing of a large amount of luck. The Mini's front-wheel drive undoubtedly helped to pull her out of a nasty skid, which Tina brought entirely under control. She was then able to direct some of her attention to the perpetrator of the outrage, with a view to coming to a halt and giving him a piece of her mind —and taking his name and address—for the most appalling piece of botched overtaking she had ever encountered.

Her rear-view mirror told her nothing about her fellow driver, save that he wore dark glasses and an absurd woolly hat, and gave no sign of recognising her presence: not even as much as a wave of apology, nor did the other attempt to slow down, but kept close upon the Mini's tail.

Furious, Tina gave a brusque hand signal to indicate that she was going to stop, and took her foot off the accelerator.

An instant later, the sturdy front end and massive fender of the other vehicle smashed into the tender panels at the rear of the little saloon and smashed them inwards. Impelled by the irresistible force of inertia, she distinctly felt her sixth and seventh cervical vertebrae click out of joint and back in again, and the Mini was ploughed forward as the speeding juggernaut rammed home a second time.

It was then Tina May knew that Death had closed upon her.

The eyas, following the shocks of impact, seemed to have shrunk to a third of her size, and was huddled, shivering with terror, upon her perch.

He had no eyes for her, being totally concerned to keep his prey moving; if the Mini slowed down and stopped, his intention would be lost. However, a couple more solid clouts to the rear and the other driver, realizing the score, put her foot down and sped away—to escape.

This was just what he wanted. He allowed the Mini to build up speed to the upper seventies. The road was as straight as a die. Still not a thing else in sight. The embankment was at its deepest and steepest: the tops of quite tall pines were almost at the level of the roadway.

He braced himself for the third and last movement in the Dance of Death.

He jammed his foot hard down: the Land-Rover picked up speed, engine opened full out.

He was attempting another side-swipe that would send the Mini spinning off the road and into the abyss below.

(Let her go, let her go! Both for her betrayal and because she was no use to him anyhow. He had had high hopes for her. She could have been his right hand—but had proved to be an empty shell. Now she had to be silenced, for she had guessed too much and might tell more. It was only natural justice: an eye for an eye, kill or be killed.)

She knew he was closing up on her; saw that he had pulled out to sweep her off the road. She could go no faster, and the other was nearly abreast again.

With nothing else on earth to do but scream, she did the next best thing and pressed the horn, and it had a particularly strident note—for a Mini. The sound of it, blasting through the shattered side window of the Land-Rover, had a more marked effect upon the eyas's screaming nerve ends, even, than the bumping and buffeting she had suffered—such is the unpredictable nature of the beast. She went totally wild: bating in the air, flapping her powerful wings, and screeching with panic. And the horn continued to blast away.

The Land-Rover was in position to ram again. Judging it to a nicety, he tensed himself to spin the wheel and end it all.

It was in that same instant that the eyas broke free!

The leash that secured her to the perch, half severed by the falling glass, snapped clean with the force of her last, mad bate. The panic-stricken predator saw the open driver's window and felt the rush of pure air coming through. Her whole endeavour was directed towards bursting out of there —to freedom.

He felt the beat of her wings; grabbed at her when her primaries slashed against his cheek, managed to secure a clumsy hold upon her tail. She screeched and clawed at the man who was impeding her. Three descending talons, commencing their downward rake on his brow near the hairline, scored three scarlet furrows down to his jaw, taking with them his right eye. His scream mingled with hers as, relinquishing his hold of the wheel and the eyas's tail, he pressed his hands to his ruined face.

The Land-Rover, uncontrolled, took a slanting course across the road and away from the Mini. It travelled for a hundred yards or so parallel to the opposite verge, then the camber of the surface took charge and inclined the front wheels to disaster.

The heavy vehicle went over the edge at something approaching eighty miles an hour nose first. And disappeared from the horrified sight of Tina May.

She pulled in a little farther on and walked back to the scene of the crash. Peering down, she saw the Land-Rover lying on its side, the driver half-spilled out of the open door, arms sprawled, head lolling on the broken neck. The dark glasses were hanging from one ear and one sightless eye was turned skywards, to where the eyas was slowly circling above, among the treetops—but not for long. Presently she wheeled and flew away, and neither the guile of a falconer nor all the lures in the world would have enticed her back.

TWELVE

The conference room on the fourth floor of the New Scotland Yard building was being painted out, so the meeting to tie up the loose ends of what was forever to remain the dossier on the Turner Syndrome was held in the anteroom of the senior officers' restaurant on the penthouse floor. Present were the deputy commissioner, who was chairing the meeting, Arkwright, Turner, and a stenographer. Tina May was there by invitation and as an accredited adviser, and the psychiatrist Heymans as an expert consultant.

The gathering sat down at 10 A.M. Coffee and biscuits were served. Heymans had not yet arrived.

"I've never known that man to be on time," observed Arkwright.

The D.C. consulted his pocket watch: he was a man of strict habits in time-keeping. "Well, I shall not hold up the meeting for Dr. Heymans," he said. "I have to be at Number Ten at noon, and the P.M. is not to be kept waiting." He tapped the table as if to translate the proceedings from a coffee break to a hard-nosed official conclave.

He glanced towards Tina, treating her to the frosty smile which he employed to mask the nervousness that always beset him in the presence of attractive women. "I should like, first of all, to congratulate Dr. May on her providential escape from a most appalling situation," he said.

"We had the entire Essex constabulary searching for her and the killer," said Arkwright. "Helicopters and all. But it wasn't enough." He glanced sidelong at her, seated as she was on his left. "We could have lost you for good," he added lugubriously.

"I'm not so easily disposed of, Derek," she said gently. "I'm a Thursday's child, with a long way to go."

The D.C. blew his nose loudly to fill the hiatus of silence that followed this tender exchange. "Let us now proceed to the evidence that came to light during the search of Farrell's premises," he said. "Arkwright—will you take over from here, please?"

"Yes, sir." Arkwright opened a folder and produced a large scribbling diary for the current year, together with a sheaf of loose notes. "Farrell the murderer—and despite his high-flown pretensions I shall persist in so describing him—was meticulous in his bookkeeping. A search of the cottage brought this to light." He held up the diary. "Not only does it contain a complete account of the proceedings of his so-called society, together with membership, a list of the victims, and who disposed of them, but also an outline of the perverted philosophy which was the basis of Farrell's activities. I will begin with the hard facts about the society:

"It was conceived in late January of this year with a meeting between Farrell and Miss Slyte. We know her to be sincerely convinced of the rightness of positive euthanasia, and when challenged she made not the slightest attempt to defend herself, offering only the baldest of statements in justification.

"A week later, Farrell met the man we know best as Norman—the ex-Marine and old lag turned strongman Edward Thomas Wain. There's a tragic irony here, for it can be said that Wain thoroughly pulled the wool over Farrell's eyes. This scoundrel listened to Farrell's harangue and, behind the high-flown talk, he saw the smoothest, easiest racket that had ever come his way in a lifetime of villainy. Farrell enrolled him in the society—and we have a note here, written only a few days before his death. I will read it to you: 'Norman is no use to the Society. He lacks the intelligence, initiative, and most of all the commitment, to serve our great cause. In the months since his induction, he has not made contact with a single subject, nor even checked with me for further advice and inspiration. Such helpers are useless. At the earliest opportunity, I shall inform him that he is expelled from the society.' " Arkwright looked around the table with a cynical smile. "In view of the fact that Norman— who you might say had become a freelance member of the society, working to his own rules—had already disposed of at least one victim and possibly more whom we shall never trace, and had at least two other women lined up for slaughter, we know that Farrell was much mistaken, on all counts, in his protégé."

"How many victims did these people dispose of?" asked Tina. "Or shall we never know for sure?"

"Quite firmly, and discounting Norman's private enterprise," replied Arkwright, "there were three. The diary tells it all most scrupulously. Miss Slyte assisted Miss Waterhouse to her death. Farrell himself drowned the suicidally depressed Mr. Foy in his bath—after he had panicked and struggled. And he also pushed Artur Tostig into oblivion.

"Furthermore, we have mute confirmation of these facts." So saying, he reached below the table and brought up a cardboard box. This held three screw-top containers in which such things as cocoa and instant coffee are vended. Unscrewing the caps, he overturned the jars, and sheafs of banknotes fluttered down on to the table top.

"The sums of two hundred and fifty, one thousand, and five thousand pounds," he said. "Being the so-called 'donations' received from Waterhouse, Foy, and Tostig respectively. And not a penny spent, but all carefully husbanded for the furtherance of the 'great cause.' Farrell may have been insane, but he was sincere with it!"

"And *who* is presuming to bandy the term 'insane' about in my absence?" No one had heard the door quietly open to admit the flamboyant figure of Dr. Heymans. He stood inside the threshold, one hand on well-tailored hip, one foot advanced like a dancing master, puckish face screwed into an expression of mock indignation. "Ah, it was the excellent Detective Chief Inspector Arkwright—and I thank you by the way, sir, for sending me a copy of your case notes. You were speaking of the unlamented Farrell. Now, as I have already told the enchanting Dr. May, this man was no more insane than any of us here . . ."

As he spoke, Heymans drifted slowly across the room towards the table and to the vacant chair that had clearly been set for him, treating the D.C. to a smile and a gracious inclination of his head *en passant*.

"From my perusal of your notes, furthermore," he continued, "I would say the same of Miss Slyte. The best construction one can put upon her motives is that she is a do-gooder. At worst, a curtain-twitching, interfering old woman of whom our suburbs provide innumerable examples from both sexes." He sat down and shot his cuffs. "Farrell, if he had lived, would have found such folk a rich source of recruitment."

"And what about the man who called himself Norman?" asked Tina. "How do you categorise him?"

Heymans allowed himself a few moments to gaze enrapt upon her before he replied. When he did, his mask had changed to Tragedy. "Criminally insane," he declared. "Amoral as to life or property: 'I want, therefore I must have; he stands in my way, therefore I will destroy him.' Farrell made a grave mistake, from his point of view, in choosing such a bestial creature."

"I think," said Tina May ruefully, "that he also had me in mind as a possible recruit."

"I can vouch for that," said Arkwright, riffling through the pages of the diary. "There is an entry relating to the occasion when he first met you, Tina, at the TV studio, and he wrote: 'The May woman is worth following up. As a pathologist, she is certain to be totally unsentimental about death. An additional bonus—she would provide an unchallengeable source of supply of killing drugs.'"

"Good God!" exclaimed the D.C., and stared at Tina with some disfavour.

"However, by the time you had lunched together, he had amended his view," said Arkwright.

"It happens, it happens," trilled Heymans. *"La donna è mobile."* He met the D.C.'s frown. "I do so beg your pardon."

"After that," said Arkwright, "he wrote: 'I may have been wrong about T.M.—unfortunately she shows a squeamishness that is quite out of character with her occupation. But I'll keep trying, if only for her usefulness in obtaining drugs.' There's more, Tina—and he did definitely go off you in a most unflattering way."

Tina shivered. "Thank heaven for that," she said with fervour.

There was further discussion, mostly concerning the minutiae of police procedure, during which Heymans constantly sought Tina's eye and once winked broadly at her. The psychiatrist's primary source of amusement appearing to be centred upon the deputy commissioner's lugubrious manner, he gave a rendering of the way in which the other conducted the meeting: mirroring his gestures and facial expressions, silently mouthing his pedantic phraseology— yet so sparely that it took a close observer to see what the twitching, the eyebrow raising, the tiny gestures were all about. Tina, who saw and understood very clearly, was obliged to look away for fear of laughing aloud. No one else, the D.C. included, appeared to notice what Heymans was up to.

It was in the winding up of the proceedings, however, that the eminent psychiatrist demonstrated to Tina, as to the others, that he was more than a lightweight clown. The D.C. posed the comment that the Turner Syndrome had demonstrated, if nothing else, the absolute folly of legalising positive euthanasia.

"You are quite right, sir," responded Heymans with a perfectly straight face. "What we have seen here is a microcosm of what would happen if that disastrous situation were to come about. The proportions are just about correct . . .

One third of those who became involved would be, like Farrell, unfulfilled creatures with the compulsion to play God. Another third would comprise the do-gooders, the busybodies—and they would also include the genuinely compassionate. Heaven protect us from such all-consuming compassion! From out of the stinking mires of human degradation would emerge the other third. The least repulsive of these would be the professional racketeers who seize upon any legislative folly—prohibition of alcohol, relaxation of gaming laws, and so forth—as a means to amass unbelievable power and wealth—oh yes, those gentry would be right in there, grafting the last penny from their victims. Below them would come animals like the unlamented Norman, along with perverts of the kind who, anticipating the happy event of Britain reintroducing capital punishment, continue to write to the Home Office, asking to be put on the list of trainee hangmen.

That's what such legislation would bring, Mr. Deputy Commissioner. We've seen it played out already with just three people running the show."

The meeting broke up at a quarter to twelve, and the D.C. was fussing to leave and keep his appointment. Tina shook hands with them all, making a point of congratulating Turner on not only being the first to spot the syndrome, but sticking with it through thick and thin.

She also accepted an early luncheon date with Derek Arkwright at Oscar's restaurant.

The closing vignette of the event took place at the door of the ante-room, where the D.C. made much of the fact, for the third time, that he was in a hurry. "I'm due at Number Ten at midday," he declared importantly, casting his eye around to make sure that everyone had heard.

"Let's share a cab, then, my dear fellow," said Heymans. "I'm lunching with the Prime Minister, too."

The continued nonreappearance of Maggie Wainwright from Scotland was explained by the receipt of a telegram on the morning that Tina was due to appear before the Medical Council. She opened it whilst hurrying over a scratch breakfast: standing up, a piece of toast in the other hand, a half-drunk cup of coffee on the top of the fridge, and the radio giving out the weather report. What she read there nearly made her drop the toast:

DR TINA MAY 18 LOCHIEL STREET CHELSEA LONDON

PROTRACTED DALLIANCE CONFIRMING THAT MUTUAL CHEMISTRY IS JUST ABOUT RIGHT WE HAVE DECIDED TO GET MARRIED IN A HURRY STOP KNOW THAT YOU WILL GIVE YOUR BLESSING STOP ALL LOVE + MAGGIE AND JOCK

The hoot of the minicab she had ordered cut short her speculations about this astonishing news till she was settled in the cab and being carried eastwards along the King's Road. It was then—after rereading the missive half-a-dozen times, and passing through innumerable shades of reaction which varied from a slight sense of betrayal by Maggie, through a curious feeling of loss, to a distinct sense of pity for both the parties involved—she came to her final, triumphant summation that, on the whole, the couple were probably made for each other. And that she—Tina—was free, free, *free* of Jock at last!

Paying off the minicab outside the offices of the Medical Council, she mounted the steps and pushed her way through the swing doors into an echoing hall. The first people she saw were Janet Barden and a bespectacled man in clerical grey whom she correctly assumed to be Jan's partner Dickie Moore.

Jan introduced them. Moore was unsmiling and earnest. "It seems," he said, "that those whom for want of a better term we must call the Prosecution have briefed a Queen's Counsel to appear before the Committee, which suggested to us that they mean business. And so . . ."

"Why, here he is," interposed Jan.

Turning to follow the direction in which Jan was looking, Tina saw a familiar smiling face.

"We've briefed Mr. Marcus Struthers to appear for you," said Dickie Moore.

"If that's all right?" said Marc Struthers, and there was the ghost of anxiety in his grey-eyed glance.

"Of course, Marc," said Tina. She clasped his hands, and he kissed her cheek. "Who else could I possibly have wished for?"

"The other side have had to work a switch," said Moore. "As you know, Struthers, they originally briefed Cobbold, Q.C., but he's gone down with Asian flu and they've now brought in Scott, Q.C." He gave the other a quizzical glance. "I believe you know him well."

Marc Struthers grinned and shrugged his broad shoulders. "Jake Scott and I have been sparring partners ever since we were both called to the Bar on the same occasion," he said, "and before then when we were doing our pupilage in the same chambers." He looked at Tina. "It will be a double triumph to confound old Jake today," he added.

The double doors into the Council Chamber opened and out filed a group of people who were clearly connected with the case that had just been heard. Tina searched their faces for a clue as to the unfortunate fellow-practitioner who had likewise been summoned to appear before his peers, but gleaned only that they all seemed quite cheerful, so there must have been an acquittal.

An elderly functionary beckoned them from the doors: "Case of Dr. May?" he whispered. "Would you please come in."

Marc took her elbow. "Tina, I won't be calling you to give evidence," he murmured. "Just maintain your look of Olympian calm. And don't worry."

One's immediate impression of the Council Chamber was that of considerable size, which might have been on account of its excellent proportions, for the high table fronting the

long windows that looked out to the grey façades of Blooms-
bury stretched the width of the room, yet barely accommo-
dated the six committee members—four men and two
women—who sat there.

Tina and her solicitors were ushered to seats at the rear of
the chamber; Struthers took his place at a long bench fronting the high table, after making a deep bow to the president
of the Committee. He then nodded to the man who shared
the far end of the bench—and Tina recognised Scott, Q.C.
from the one occasion when she had given expert evidence
in a criminal case where he had prosecuted.

There was some muttering between the president and his
near neighbours, and then the former—white-haired, tall,
and thin as a crane, and carrying an air of distinction with
consummate ease—smiled down at the prosecuting counsel.

"Ah, Mr. Scott," he purred, "if you would be so kind as to
give us a lead and commence the proceedings, please."

Scott got to his feet. "Mr. President, ladies and gentlemen," he said, "in this hearing, my learned friend Mr.
Struthers appears for Dr. Tina Patricia May, and I for the
Medical Council. The deposition of the mortuary attendant
Skerrit not being disputed by the defence, Skerrit will not be
called, and I understand that my learned friend is not calling
Dr. May. It follows that the committee's decision must rest
upon pleadings by myself and Mr. Struthers." He looked
questioningly at the president.

"Please proceed, Mr. Scott," came the response.

It was then, while scanning the faces of the committee,
that Tina saw that all save one had eyes only for Jake Scott as
he began his peroration—and the exception was the unsa-
voury countenance of Warburton-Fosse: pale, with a pur-
plish, tapirlike nose and hooded, shifty eyes that stared
across at her with malevolent triumph.

Holding her head up high, she very pointedly looked
away.

". . . and it is my submission, Mr. President, ladies and
gentlemen," said Scott, "that we have here a deliberate *sup-*

pressio veri, certainly for personal, and possibly also for political reasons, for Dr. May, by her own admission, is a family friend of the dead girl's parents.

"Leaving that aspect aside for a moment, this suppression of the dead girl's condition casts grave doubts upon the accuracy of the rest of the forensic evidence. We are told that the deceased had not been taking drugs; it is certain that her companions, even the driver of the car, had been taking drugs. We are told that the dead girl had not been drinking heavily; her companions, the driver included, were well over the permitted limit of alcohol in the blood . . ."

Trapped! . . .

Tina May, hideously aware that Warburton-Fosse's eyes were still upon her, had the clear impression of a net closing in all round, as Scott's smooth, eminently reasonable-sounding voice wove the tissue of speculative fantasy from out of nowhere, allowing it to settle in gossamer folds about her, binding her tightly in a web of lies that was hardening with every uncaring moment to bonds of steel.

Why doesn't someone stop him? she cried inside. *Marc . . .*

But Marc Struthers was gazing stonily ahead. He stifled a yawn, and scratched his ear with elaborate casualness. No help from that quarter.

". . . Returning to Dr. May's personal involvement," Scott was saying, "it has nowhere been denied that she has dined regularly with the Harknesses and is on first name terms with both the Member of Parliament and cabinet minister and his wife." He paused—as if to allow Harkness's elevated status to sink into his listeners' consciousness. "I do not wish to pursue this particular issue any further, save to point out that the providential release of Dr. May's *suppressio veri* placed the minister in a most deleterious light—and you may think, Mr. President, ladies and gentlemen, that the possibility of such a risk to her friend's reputation motivated Dr. May to the *suppressio veri* in the first place.

"And that, Mr. President, ladies and gentlemen, is my plea." So saying, Jake Scott sat down.

"Thank you, Mr. Scott," responded the President. He glanced down at Marc Struthers and smiled benignly. "Mr. Struthers?"

"Thank you, Mr. President." Struthers rose and panned along the row of faces before him. He had watched carefully during his opponent's address, and had observed that the glances of the two women on the committee had several times strayed thoughtfully towards Tina May—which he took to be a good sign, and that the President was obviously a thoroughly well-intentioned old chap. He had not overlooked the malevolent attention of Warburton-Fosse.

"Mr. President, ladies and gentlemen," he began, "I have seldom heard such thin gruel of argument served to a distinguished body as my learned friend dished up to you just now, and I will totally deny—nay, ignore!—the trumped-up imputations laid at my client's door, and concentrate upon the essential issue.

"The essential issue is why Dr. May chose to omit the fact of the girl's pregnancy from her report. Putting aside such specious considerations as her supposed concern for Mr. Harkness's career and the government's standing in the country—and what have we left?

"We have a dead fifteen-year-old girl lying on a mortuary slab. An innocent abroad in fast company. We know she was innocent because she had neither taken alcohol in any quantity nor drugs at all. But she was three months pregnant.

"Mr. President, ladies and gentlemen, you are all members of the medical profession. You must often—even more frequently than I—a lawyer—come into contact with this problem of young girls who 'fall.' I put it to you, members of the committee, what is generally the nature and quality of these young unfortunates—are they for the most part 'good' girls or 'bad' girls?

"I will answer that for you"—and his voice took on a note of sober concern—"it isn't the 'bad' girls who mostly fall—they're too smart, they know all the answers. It's the 'good' girls—the poor little innocents abroad—who fall."

His declaration was greeted by nods of grave agreement from some of the committee—including both women.

Struthers waited for his remarks to have their maximum impact before he resumed in the same serious vein.

"That," he said, "is exactly how it was with fifteen-year-old Dawn Harkness. Taking into account her age and state, Dr. May shrewdly reckoned that this innocent had not dared to tell her parents about her condition—*and this fact was later borne out!*"

He paused for a moment. "So there you have it. Dr. May's so-called *suppressio veri* was motivated by no more than decency and tact—to spare further hurt and regret on the part of the parents, and to shield a dead innocent.

"That, Mr. President, is the beginning, the middle, and the ending of it. And all I have to say."

He sat down.

After some murmuring amongst the committee, the president indicated that the chamber was to be vacated of all save themselves. Tina waited for Struthers to draw abreast of her then she took his hand and they walked out together.

"Thank you, Marc," she murmured. "If they were to erase my name from the Register, if they were to hang, draw and quarter me, I couldn't have had a better defender."

"You'll be okay," he replied, and squeezed her hand.

The committee was in deliberation for no more than five minutes before the usher appeared and readmitted them. Tina went back to her place, not daring to look at the members at the high table, since she knew the old courthouse lore about jurors avoiding the prisoner's eye when they have found him guilty.

A rustle of papers, and she heard the president say: "Dr. May, will you please rise?"

This she did, and to her instant joy, saw that they were looking at her—all save one: Warburton-Fosse was scowling down at his hands.

"Dr. May," said the president, "I have to inform you that the committee have carefully considered the complaint brought against you, and are of the opinion that there is no evidence to support the same.

"Indeed," he added, with a surprisingly venomous side-long scowl in the direction of Warburton-Fosse, "the over-whelming majority of the committee is of the opinion that the complaint should never have been brought!

"That terminates the case."

Tina caught Marc Struthers's eye and mouthed a "Thank you."

Home . . .

And home was a very lonely place that night. Maggie gone. Jock gone (could she *really* be so lucky?). And now this . . .

"This" was an invitation to the wedding of Miss Jessica Ruth Rothstein and Mr. Jeremy Hardcourt Cook, to be held at St. Margaret's, Westminster on such-and-such, reception to follow at the Ritz. And no mention of parental endorse-ment, support, or presence, so the two of them were launch-ing themselves out into the stormy sea of matrimony with nothing but each other and a comfortable fortune.

"And I have a notion," said Tina, aloud, "that they will make it. What did Jessica say?: 'Watch this space in five years' time!' Well, we'll do just that—and meantime, I'll be there at St. Margaret's throwing rice and rose leaves for six. You bet!"

There came a knock on the back door. Not many people save tradesmen used the back door. Tina opened it upon a small girl of about seven or eight who was huddled up in an oversized mackintosh against the streaming rain.

"Hello," said Tina. "Come on in before you get soaked. Aren't you the girl from over the garden wall? What can I do for you?"

Clearly, the child had been crying. "It—it's about the little cat," she said.

"What little cat?" asked Tina.

"Mummy says he'll have to go now that Sukie's having another litter," said the child. "Only no one wants him 'cos they say he's so ugly. So—so he'll be put down!" She began to cry again, and it was while she was groping for a handkerchief that the mackintosh fell open and a smallish ginger form descended lightly from within its folds and landed four-square at Tina's feet.

It looked up at her, opened its mouth, and gave a loud and insistent wail.

"I don't believe it!" breathed Tina. "There's no such thing as transmigration—or *is* there?"

"Will you have him?" pleaded the child. "He's only six months, but he's house-trained. But we never gave him a name," she added sadly.

"His name's You," said Tina, her eyes prickling. "I knew his father well."

Mrs. Iris Carruthers sat in an overstuffed easy chair in her overdecorated drawing room at the Grange, a glass of gin-and-water at her plump elbow and a small cigar clenched between her painted lips. A pink telephone occupied the corner of the card table set beside the chair, and she glanced at it from time to time as she dealt herself into another game of patience.

The centre of the card table was occupied by banknotes of twenty-pound denomination in five piles of fifty notes each —making a total of five thousand pounds. Mrs. Carruthers's eyes occasionally strayed in that direction, also.

Though living alone in that vast house, she was serenely happy, for she had a recent memory to buoy her up—that and the recollection of how she had defied her stepson and that bank manager and got what she wanted.

Happy, though all alone; needing nothing from the outside, neither television nor radio, newspapers or idle gossip.

She had her cards, and her telephone, and the money.

And some day—one day soon—Norman would ring her.

Just as he'd promised.